"I'd better go.

"No," Katherine whispered. "Don't."

"You know what will happen if I stay."

"I know."

Stephen kissed her again. "You said—just coffee."

"A woman has a right to change her mind, doesn't she?"

"As long as she doesn't lose it entirely in the process. Do you honestly understand what you're doing, Katherine?" His voice held a rough edge.

"Yes!" It was a reckless lie, and she knew it, but for the first time in her life she was determined to act on the impulse.

Leigh Michaels started her fiction-writing career when she was in elementary school, by making up new endings to favorite books in order to put herself to sleep at night. And though those experiments in story-writing were never committed to paper, she says plotting them out was good practice for her ten years of writing romance novels.

She has also written newspaper features, magazine articles, a textbook, short stories, poems and—she estimates—two tons of letters. She likes hearing from readers at P.O. Box 935, Ottumwa, Iowa, 52501-0935.

Books by Leigh Michaels

HARLEQUIN ROMANCE
3141—PROMISE ME TOMORROW
3160—TEMPORARY MEASURES
3171—GARRETT'S BACK IN TOWN
3184—OLD SCHOOL TIES
3214—THE BEST-MADE PLANS
3233—THE UNEXPECTED LANDLORD

HARLEQUIN PRESENTS
1107—CLOSE COLLABORATION
1147—A NEW DESIRE
1245—ONCE AND FOR ALWAYS
1266—WITH NO RESERVATIONS

SAFE IN MY HEART
Leigh Michaels

Harlequin Books

TORONTO • NEW YORK • LONDON
AMSTERDAM • PARIS • SYDNEY • HAMBURG
STOCKHOLM • ATHENS • TOKYO • MILAN
MADRID • WARSAW • BUDAPEST • AUCKLAND

ISBN 0-373-03248-X

Harlequin Romance first edition February 1993

SAFE IN MY HEART

CHAPTER ONE

THE ROOM WAS midnight-dark except for the burglar's small flashlight flicking on at random intervals.

At the side of the room, Katherine Whitman sat stiffly upright in her straight, uncomfortable chair, fingers clenched on the edges of the seat. She was staring, eyes wide, toward the center of the room, straining to hear the occasional whisper of sound that told her where the burglar was. There was nothing to see between those irregular flashes of light, but she stared anyway in a futile effort to make out the image of what she knew was there.

Total darkness could do strange things to a person, Katherine reminded herself. It interfered with one's balance, since there was no landmark to relate to. It was almost smothering, like a blanket of warm fog. And it played games with the mind. Deprived of external stimuli, her brain insisted on making up its own data, so she actually believed that she could see a flicker of movement and shape and color as the burglar drew nearer.

The instantaneous, ludicrous urge to run had passed, but that didn't eliminate Katherine's longing to move, to cross one slim knee over the other, to scratch her nose, even to take a deep breath. Her orders, however, had been very clear. And any minute now—no, any *second* it would be over, anyway. . . .

A tiny red light blinked once, up in the corner of the room, seeming as bright in the blackness as if it had been the sun rising, and a millisecond later a siren began to shriek above her head. Instinctively, Katherine closed her eyes just as spotlights—so powerful that she could hear the pop of the filaments as they flared into life—illuminated the burglar where he crouched in the center of the room.

He flung himself facedown and pounded a frustrated fist on the floor. "Dammit, would you shut that thing off?" he yelled, and the siren died into blessed silence. The room lights came on, the powerful spots flicked off, and Katherine took her hands away from her ears and blinked as her eyes readjusted to normal light.

The claustrophobic feel of the room had faded away along with the total darkness. This was not the small, cramped office it had seemed during the exercise, but an enormous, warehouselike space. The model room the burglar had been attempting to invade was just one of a half dozen sets in HomeSafe's test laboratory. And Katherine hadn't been alone in the dark, either; every chair in the observers' gallery was occupied.

The man sitting beside her finished the notation he was writing in his leather-bound notebook, capped his fountain pen and put it away in the breast pocket of his jacket, then strode over to the black-clad figure on the floor.

"Well, Jake," Stephen Osborne asked politely, "what do you think of our new motion detector now?"

The burglar rolled onto his back and stared up at the man standing over him. "You told me you'd built a pet alley into the damned thing, Steve," he accused. "You said the dead space was big enough so the guard dogs could wander around without setting the alarms off. You lied to me—"

"Lied? Not at all. Of course there's a pet alley, exactly where I told you it was. But you, my friend, are slightly larger than a German shepherd. More importantly, your profile's different."

The burglar sat up and tugged off his gloves. "Do you mean to say your new system recognized, in the dark, that I don't have a tail?"

"Something like that." Stephen held a hand out.

The burglar grabbed it and leapt lightly to his feet. "And I suppose that's all you're going to tell me."

Stephen's dark eyebrows lifted. "Of course. It's a trade secret. All you need to know is that it'll protect your customers even if they don't understand exactly how it works."

The burglar pulled the black stocking mask off his head and ran his fingers through his disheveled hair. They were a study in contrasts as they stood there shoulder-to-shoulder—Stephen Osborne, just a shade over six feet, impeccably tailored in silver-gray with a silk shirt and a hand-sewn tie, every dark brown hair in place. And Jake Holland, an inch shorter and a bit slighter in frame, in his black turtleneck and slacks, ruffled and dusty and every inch the cat burglar.

They were a strange pair of friends, Katherine found herself thinking.

A young woman standing nearby, one of a half dozen sales representatives who'd attended the test, turned to Katherine with a shiver. "Jake Holland really gets into this stuff, doesn't he? He could run these tests just as well with the lights on, but he insists on the darkness and the black clothes and all. The man gives me the creeps."

Katherine shrugged. "Any good security consultant wants test conditions to be as much like the real situation as possible. I wouldn't want to run into Jake in a dark alley when he's in costume, but he's harmless, really."

Stephen Osborne put a casual hand on Katherine's shoulder. "Of course he's harmless. Jake's a frustrated cloak-and-dagger type, that's all. He ended up in the security business only because the CIA wouldn't take him."

"Come on, Osborne," Jake protested. "You're just saying rude things because I beat the sensors on your windows this time."

Stephen frowned. "I know. We'll have to work on that. Katherine, if you're going back to the office, would you put this on my desk?" He handed her the leather-bound notebook. "I'm taking Jake to lunch so I can pick his brains. Oh, and would you ask Irene to reserve a table for two at The Pinnacle tonight? Ten o'clock should be safe."

Katherine frowned a little. "Safe?"

Stephen nodded. "In case the play runs long. We're seeing *Henry* the some-number-or-other."

And he obviously didn't care what number it was, Katherine thought. That meant his companion tonight would probably be Hilary Clayton, for she, not Stephen, was the Shakespeare fan. Which meant his table had better be ready the moment the play was over, because the gorgeous and self-assured Hilary did not like to be kept waiting. And *that* meant Katherine had better explain it all very carefully to the sometimes hapless Irene—or else go ahead and make the reservation herself. "I'll look after it, Stephen."

Stephen put his index finger under Katherine's chin and tipped her face up. "You don't have to. Remember? You're not a secretary anymore—Irene is."

"Getting a table at The Pinnacle on a Friday night isn't a matter to leave to the average secretary," she pointed out.

He smiled down at her, his dark brown eyes dancing with golden lights. "What's the matter, Katherine? Are you aiming for another promotion by offering to take on even more executive responsibility? You might as well not bother—there's nothing for you to move up to except my job, and I'm not ready to retire." He and Jake Holland left the security lab and vanished down the hall.

The sales representative shook her head. "Honestly, Katherine, I don't know how you stand working for him."

"Stephen?" She was startled. "He's a great boss."

"I don't doubt that. But how do you manage to keep from exploding in flames every time he looks at you? Take the way he smiles, for instance."

Katherine's jaw dropped. "Are you feeling all right, Diane? Exposure to total darkness affects some people strangely. Stephen has a very pleasant smile, yes. It's one of the nicest things about him, but—"

Diane was staring over the tops of her half-glasses. "All right," she said abruptly. "Who is he?"

"What on earth do you mean?"

"The man who can keep you from noticing that Stephen Osborne exudes sex appeal."

Katherine shrugged. "I don't have any idea what you're talking about." The fact that she wasn't quite telling the truth tugged at her conscience. No one knew about her and Travis, and he insisted that was the way it had to remain for the present. It wouldn't be much longer, though. If the sales figures for last month ended up as Travis expected they would, and he was once again HomeSafe's top salesman . . .

Diane was watching her doubtfully.

"Look," Katherine said, "you wouldn't think in terms of sex appeal if you had to work with the man all the time. Don't you know the office law that says no man is a hero to his secretary?"

Diane mulled that one over. "But you're not anymore. You're his personal assistant."

"Technically, I never was his secretary. But the same principle applies." Katherine knelt beside her chair to gather up the folders she'd tucked safely underneath, in case Stephen had wanted information on any of the sensors or circuitry they'd been testing that morning. "Why wasn't Travis Baker here, Diane?" she asked carelessly. "I thought he wanted to see this demonstration."

"He's got a problem with one of his accounts in Boulder, I guess. He won't be back till late this afternoon."

Katherine tried not to let herself feel disappointed. His absence really made no difference; even if Travis had attended, they couldn't have gone out for lunch. She sighed. All this caution seemed so unnecessary. What harm was there in being seen together now and then? But Travis was being especially careful these days.

"Is he married?" Diane asked.

Katherine bit her tongue. She'd almost replied that of course Travis wasn't married. "Who do you mean?"

"Who do you think? The man in your life you're being so secretive about. Don't worry, I won't tell anyone."

Katherine put Stephen's notebook on top of the folders. "If I was to get involved with a man, I certainly wouldn't choose one who was married. Any man who'd mess around behind his wife's back wouldn't stop for long even if he happened to change wives, and I want better than that for myself." She smiled at the quizzical look on Diane's face. "And no, that doesn't mean I've been burned by a married man, either. So why don't you stop speculating about my romantic history and go sell security systems? There's a lot more profit in that for both of us."

Diane shook her head in disbelief, but she went away.

Katherine stayed to talk to the head of the testing division about the next system to be installed in the model room. By the time she got back to the suite of executive offices in the front wing of the sprawling complex, it was well into the lunch hour; Irene had left her desk and locked the office door. Katherine's arms were aching from the weight of the file folders, and as she balanced them and tried to manage her key, her hand slipped and the folders scattered over the carpet.

Muttering a couple of words under her breath, she stooped to retrieve them. Stephen's leather-bound notebook had landed at her feet, open to the notes he'd been taking earlier. It was incredible, Katherine thought, that even in total darkness his writing was so neat it looked as if he'd had a desk lamp beside him.

Not only does he set female employees on fire, she mused, *but he can see in the dark, too. I should rush right down and tell Diane that bit of news!*

She left the stack of folders for Irene to file and went on into Stephen's office, which was large and luxurious and so quiet that the sound of her own breathing seemed intrusive. It smelled good, too—a mix of leather and coffee and after-shave and the barest hint of cigar tobacco, no doubt still lingering from the chairman of the board's most recent visit.

She put Stephen's notebook squarely on the center of his desk and wasted a couple of minutes gazing out at the Denver skyline. Today it looked particularly wonderful; last night's thunderstorm had cleared the summer air, and the skyline was crisp and clear and distinct in the distance. A rare sight in mid-July, when there was usually a humid haze over the city.

The big leather chair was turned toward the window, as if Stephen had also been gazing out over the city just before he went down to the lab. Katherine didn't blame him. She, too, could think more clearly while looking at that glorious view.

Oh, well, back to business. She turned and walked the short distance to her own office, settled at her desk, and called The Pinnacle for Stephen's dinner reservation. The mere mention of his name won a warm response from the maître d' and a promise that Mr. Osborne's table would be ready no matter when he wanted it.

Obviously, Stephen tipped very well indeed. Or else that charm Diane had been talking of worked on waiters, too.

Katherine smiled. Diane had made it sound as if Stephen Osborne possessed a magnetism that drew women irresistibly into his power. And it was true that there was no lack of women in his life. Irene might be the one who had to keep his calendar straight, but Katherine certainly saw it often enough to know how frequently he was dating and who he was seeing. It wasn't a short list.

Not that there was much variety there. They all seemed to be the cool and glamorous type, like Hilary

Clayton—elegant and fashionable and suspiciously perfect.

In fact, the mere thought of Hilary Clayton as Stephen's love slave was enough to cause whoops of laughter, once Katherine let her imagination slip the leash and roam free. It simply wasn't possible to picture Hilary's perfectly coiffed blond hair rumpled in the aftermath of lovemaking. But Stephen seemed to appreciate that icy perfection, so who was Katherine to question the attraction?

There was certainly no question about what Hilary saw in him; she was the kind who would have been attracted to Stephen Osborne even if he'd been two feet tall with warts on his nose, just because he was Rafe Osborne's son and he owned a good chunk of Home-Safe. For Hilary, the fact that he was undeniably good-looking, generous, and had a smile that could melt the North Pole would be frosting on the cake....

"Cut it out," Katherine told herself. Diane's flight of fancy might be silly, but it was proving to be infectious.

Katherine went to get herself a cup of coffee, wrinkled her nose at the muddy-looking brew, and started a fresh pot. While she waited, she flipped idly through the morning mail that lay stacked on the corner of Irene's desk.

She wasn't exactly surprised that Diane's question had come up, though. She supposed talk was inevitable; when a young, attractive and, to all appearances, unattached woman went to work for a young, attractive, play-the-field man, few people would believe there was nothing more than business in the wind.

She'd considered the possibility of gossip a full year ago, when Rafe Osborne had announced his retirement and Stephen had taken over his father's position as president of HomeSafe, offering Katherine the job as his personal assistant.

But she'd never discussed it with Stephen, of course; it would have been ridiculous, and even insulting, to imply that the two of them might not be able to work together without sex interfering. And of course she'd been correct not to worry; in the entire year since she'd become his assistant there had never been an off-color comment or a too personal question or—heaven forbid—a pass to be deflected. They were professionals, after all, and work came first.

She'd attempted to explain that principle to Travis— without success. It didn't matter whether or not people knew about them, she'd argued. As long as they continued to do their jobs well, no one cared about their personal lives.

But most people didn't think that way, he had told her. His fellow salesmen would assume he was trying to use his connections to improve himself, if they knew he was dating the president's assistant, It might even put Katherine's own job at risk if Stephen didn't like the idea. And even though Katherine thought he was mad to suspect that Stephen would care one way or the other, she'd reluctantly agreed to say nothing until Travis got his hoped-for promotion.

They'd keep their relationship quiet until the new sales director was named. It was bound to be Travis. And then...

But it was difficult, Katherine admitted as she took her coffee back to her office. Sometimes she just wanted to fling open her window and shout to the world that she loved Travis Baker. It was stupid, she told herself, to wonder sometimes if he was being so secretive because down deep he was ashamed of her....

The door of her office opened. She started guiltily, and coffee splashed over the side of the mug and onto the papers spread on her desk blotter. She grabbed a tissue and began mopping up the mess.

"Daydreaming?" Rafe Osborne said pleasantly. "I didn't know you had it in you, Katherine."

She shot an aggrieved look at the chairman of the board and founder of HomeSafe, then turned her attention back to wiping coffee off the schematics of their opposition's newest security system.

Rafe tugged a chair forward, sat down and propped his feet up on the corner of her desk, ankles crossed. He was, as usual, chewing on an unlit cigar.

Katherine thought, rather irritably, that no one could possibly look less like the stereotyped chairman of a major corporation than Rafe Osborne. He was a husky bear of a man, well into his sixties, with no inclination to try to hide the marks left by a life that hadn't always been easy. He was more comfortable in Polo shirts than in suits, in bars rather than in exclusive clubs, and now that he was retired, no longer saw any reason to play by corporate rules. His hair hadn't been cut lately and his eyebrows were threateningly bushy. Certainly few people would have guessed that this abrupt, brusque man and the sophisticated new president of HomeSafe were father and son.

Rafe Osborne's style left most people in awe of him, but Katherine sometimes suspected that underneath all the sharp edges he was a marshmallow, and the bluster was simply his way to keep the rest of the world from finding out. He had, for instance, never raised his voice to her in the two years since she'd gone to work as his secretary.

He removed the cigar from his mouth. "I'm proud of you, Katherine. Most of the world's best ideas have come from someone's thoughts wandering."

She patted the last page dry and laid it aside, hoping the coffee stains wouldn't interfere with the small print. "And, of course, you're including yourself?"

"Absolutely. Being a security guard gives a man a lot of time to think between making his rounds. Sooner or later, he starts to dream up ways to make the job easier, and before he knows it he's sitting at a desk telling other people what to do. But that's old news. What's going on around this place?"

"You missed the tests of the new motion detector this morning."

Rafe shook his head. "Didn't miss it a bit—I just didn't come. With Steve and Jake Holland, it's not really product testing, you know. They're caught up in a life-size video game."

Katherine smiled. "You're right. They're just like little boys, laying traps for each other and trying to prove who's got more skill."

Rafe nodded. "That's why I went fishing instead. At least it's a civilized pastime. So how *did* the test go?"

"That's why you're here, isn't it? You expect me to give you the condensed version."

Rafe grinned. "Of course. You're my favorite spy."

She told him briefly about the test. He listened in silence, chewing on the cigar, and for a couple of long minutes afterward he stared thoughtfully at the ceiling—thinking, she was fairly certain, of the window sensors that had failed to perform as expected in this morning's trial.

Katherine had learned long ago not to disturb him at times like these, so she sat quietly, drinking her coffee and wondering what was going on behind those half-hooded brown eyes. She was not surprised when he didn't enlighten her. Instead, he took his feet off the corner of her desk and said, "Come on, I'll buy you lunch."

"As a reward for a good espionage job?" She shook her head reluctantly. "I can't. I've got loads of work to do."

"It can't be that busy around here. I just poked my head into Steve's office, and not only is Steve not there, but his desk is so clear you could land airplanes on it."

"He took Jake to lunch. Besides, heavy thinking is his job. Mine is doing the paperwork after he finishes thinking."

"Then he ought to give you the big desk. Anyway, he can't force you to stop eating. Or playing, either—*he* certainly fits in enough time for it."

Katherine smiled. "You're being contradictory, Rafe. If truly great ideas come from idle thought..."

"Doesn't mean he can't be sitting down in his office encouraging it." Rafe sounded a bit disgruntled. "Or he could go fishing—that at least gives a man a chance to think. But not Steve. If it isn't handball and tennis, it's weekends at Winter Park. Skiing is one thing. I think it's a crazy sport myself, and I haven't any idea how both my kids developed a love for it, but—"

Katherine decided that he probably hadn't thought it through, or he would have understood. Stephen's fondness for the slopes sprang from his unquenchable energy. For Rafe's daughter, Sherry, however, the attraction was another matter altogether. Katherine suspected that Sherry was more interested in the dozens of eligible young men to be found at the après-ski parties than she was in the snow.

Sherry's young, Katherine thought charitably. She'll settle down someday.

"You know, I've always wondered what Steve finds to do up there when there's no snow." Rafe sounded honestly puzzled.

Katherine looked at him in surprise and opened her mouth to answer, then decided that she'd rather not be the one who explained the facts of life to Rafe. It wasn't as if she actually knew anything, anyway, because Stephen was very discreet about his private affairs. And if his father hadn't already guessed that Stephen wasn't always alone when he used the family condo at Winter Park, Katherine wasn't about to share her speculations on the matter.

Instead, she reached into the top desk drawer for her calendar. "He hasn't said anything about going up this weekend," she murmured. "I wonder if I should call the condo office just in case, or wait till he gets back to ask him." He wouldn't be going till tomorrow anyway, she reminded herself. Unless, of course, he was planning to take Hilary along after dinner at The Pinnacle. The drive was only an hour or so; it would be a perfectly reasonable thing to do on a July night.

Rafe was shaking his head. "Not this weekend. Sherry's having a party at the penthouse tomorrow."

"And Stephen's actually going? That's a twist." She let the calendar slide back into the drawer.

"It's a different sort of party than Sherry's usual. You're coming, aren't you?"

Katherine said carefully, "I didn't know I was invited. In fact, this is the first I've heard about a party."

Rafe frowned. "Is that so? I'm sure I put your name on the guest list."

"It's not a company party, surely?"

"Oh, no—just friends and a few HomeSafe people who had to be included."

Katherine wondered in which of those categories Rafe placed her.

He flashed her a smile. "Actually," he confided, "I'm the one who's technically giving the party this time. And I had hidden reasons for asking you."

"More espionage?" Katherine asked dryly.

"Not exactly. I was hoping you'd help keep an eye on the waiters. You know the kind of thing caterers do if they think nobody's watching. So if I could just count on you to keep them honest...."

Katherine forced back a smile. For a man who'd built a brilliant brainstorm into a multimillion-dollar company, Rafe could be incredibly cheap sometimes. "All right. I'm not doing anything else, so I'll come and supervise. But you should feel extremely guilty, Rafe."

"Oh, I do," he said earnestly. "But I'll make it up to you. If you can prevent the bartenders from drinking every third bottle of champagne, I'll—"

"Champagne?" It wasn't an idle question; in Katherine's experience, any party Rafe was hosting was far more likely to include fifteen-year-old Scotch whisky.

"Crates of champagne," he said. "Not the cheap stuff, either, but then what choice do I have? Fortunately for me, a party like this only comes once in a girl's lifetime."

Katherine raised an eyebrow.

"You know better than to ask, don't you? Oh, what the hell, I'll tell you. Sherry would kill me because it's supposed to be a surprise, but I know you can keep a secret. It's her engagement party.''

Katherine blinked, and then told herself she was being unfair. Sherry was old enough to know her own mind; she'd finished college last spring. It was her behavior that made her seem so much younger than her actual years.

"How lovely for her," she said sincerely. "I had no idea she was serious about anyone."

"Well, you're not the only one who didn't. That's how I know she means it this time. She wasn't blathering on about this one every minute, not till he'd asked the question. You know him, too, of course."

Katherine tried to remember the last time she'd encountered Sherry. The girl popped into the office now and then to see Stephen, but she was always alone. And Katherine didn't move in the same social circles, so it was hardly likely that she knew any of Sherry's young men.

"He works for HomeSafe," Rafe went on.

Katherine shook her head. "Sorry to disappoint you, Rafe, but I don't know every one of your employees."

HomeSafe had a thousand workers at the four factories in Colorado, and dozens more sales and service representatives scattered halfway across the country. Katherine might be the president's personal assistant, but there were people in this very building she'd never met. Sherry's fiancé could be any one of them.

There was certainly no reason for the prickle of dread that was running with painful slowness along Katherine's nerves.

"Oh, you know this one, I'm sure. He's the best salesman we've got at the moment," Rafe assured her.

And then she knew. She wanted to shut Rafe out, to put her hands over her ears and deny what he was going to say. But she couldn't. She had no defense against the blow that was about to descend on her.

"He's going to be our new sales manager, too," Rafe said with satisfaction. "So, at least my little girl hasn't chosen some fly-by-night. Travis Baker—you know him, don't you, Katherine?"

CHAPTER TWO

IT WAS SHOCK, Katherine supposed, but it was as if she were standing across the room, watching herself absorb the blow instead of feeling it firsthand. She could almost see the color drain out of her face, leaving the sprinkling of freckles across her nose looking like muddy pools. Her body shrank back into the chair under the impact of Rafe's words.

It's a good thing she'd been sitting down when the blow hit, an inner voice observed with icy detachment. If she'd been standing, she would probably have fallen as hard as a logged tree.

Rafe walked over to the window. "I suppose people will think Steve gave him the job because of Sherry," he mused. "He didn't, of course."

No, Katherine thought. Of course he hadn't. The only thing that mattered to Stephen was how the job was done; she'd known that all along, deep inside her heart. Why had she let Travis convince her otherwise? He'd seemed so certain that dating him openly would put her job at risk...but all it had really endangered was his pursuit of bigger game. Travis would be a capable sales manager, Katherine was convinced of that. But why had it never occurred to her that his ambition went far beyond that relatively minor job?

Because you're a patsy, Katherine Whitman, she told herself bluntly.

"I'll say this for the young man," Rafe went on. "He asked Sherry to hold off announcing anything until it was certain he'd be the one to get the sales job. He's unusually modest for someone in that end of the business, that's sure."

And he's a viper in your bosom, Katherine wanted to tell Rafe. *Get rid of him before it's too late—*

But she bit her tongue and said nothing. If she told Rafe anything of the sort, he would want the details, and despite that easygoing manner of his where Katherine was concerned, he was capable of squeezing her like a sponge until he got them. And what could Katherine say that would sound like anything other than an outraged, jealous female, overreacting to the fact that the man she wanted preferred another woman?

She could show Rafe no proof of promises made and broken. Travis had never given her a ring. They'd never set a wedding date. Soon, he'd said, they would be free to talk about all that, but until then it would be wasted effort. He'd never even suggested that he move into her apartment; he'd kept his own and let her talk of the day when they would look for a larger one, together. Oh, how careful he had been!

Rafe seemed to shake himself out of a mood. "Well, I'll see you at the party, then. Eight o'clock tomorrow, the penthouse. Unless you've changed your mind about having lunch."

She tapped her coffee cup. "This is lunch." Mercifully, her hand was steady, and her voice didn't shake.

Rafe rolled his eyes heavenward. "Women. Sherry's dieting to get into a size smaller wedding gown, and you're working yourself to death. Bad judgment, both of you."

Katherine watched him leave. "You can say that again, Rafe," she muttered. "Both of us are fools—and over the same man."

She wanted to put her head down on her desk and huddle there like an ostrich retreating from the world. But at any moment Irene would be back, or Stephen—and she didn't want to explain what had made her so suddenly ill. On the other hand, if she could make her story convincing enough, not even Rafe would be expecting her to show up at Sherry's party tomorrow.

But if her story wasn't unshakable, people might begin asking questions. And whether the attitude behind those questions was compassionate, or simply idle, or downright nosy, it really didn't matter; once attention was focused on her, her folly would become common gossip.

A wave of nausea threatened to choke her, and she realized that in order to prevent talk, she was going to have to attend the engagement party. She would have to smile and congratulate the lucky couple. She would have to wish Travis the best—or have her own idiocy exposed, discussed, and enjoyed in the company lunchroom.

She was no longer such a fool as to think it wouldn't happen, either. She might have been innocent enough last week to believe that no one at HomeSafe cared what she did, but not after Diane's speculations this morning. If there was the slightest hint of scandal—and being the other woman in Sherry Osborne's romance was just about as scandalous as one could get at Home-Safe—there'd be no end to the gossip.

By midafternoon, she'd managed to pull herself together somewhat, and she even dared leave her office for the ladies' room down the hall so she could check out the damage. She still looked as if she'd picked up the wrong bottle of makeup that morning, one that was three shades darker than usual. "In fact," she told herself dispassionately, "you look as if you belong in a drawer at the morgue." She tried to practice her smile; her face felt like corrugated cardboard.

Stephen Osborne was leaning over her desk when she finally returned, rummaging through the papers she'd scattered there. "I don't know how you ever manage to keep things straight," he muttered.

Katherine brushed past him and slid into her chair so that the sunlight would be at her back rather than spotlighting her face. "I can't, when you insist on coming in to houseclean." Her voice was a bit on the husky side, but she congratulated herself that it sounded normal enough to get by. Certainly there was nothing unusual about Stephen's complaint; at least once a week he stirred up the contents of her desk, usually searching for something that was in plain view right on top.

He grinned at her, but he didn't stop riffling through her papers.

Katherine stared for a long moment at the gold sparkle in his eyes, the white gleam of perfect teeth. Ordinarily enough, she would smile back, forgiving him even if he had messed up her entire afternoon's work. Today, however, with her sense of humor gone AWOL, she was in no mood for his little foibles.

She fiddled with a pen and looked down at the nearest sheet of paper, not even registering what it was. Her hair swung forward in a golden brown mass, shielding her face.

Stephen pulled out a paper-clipped set of pages and thumbed through them. Katherine glanced up and saw the coffee stains on the top sheet.

"If you're looking for the schematics for the competition's new security system," she said crisply, "that's my set. Irene made a photocopy for you. And I told the lab to install the whole package so we can start testing it in the middle of next week."

"Great. What would I do without you, Katherine?" But he didn't, as she had hoped, go away. "That's not what I was looking for, though. I made some notes on a new twist in our premiere system, and I've mislaid them." He put the pages back in the pile on the corner of her desk.

She shook her head, interested in spite of herself. "Stephen, there are never more than three pieces of paper on your desk at any time. How could you lose one of them?"

"I thought perhaps you'd picked it up by accident, or it might have got mixed in with something else. It was just a sketch—it wouldn't make much sense if you didn't know what it was supposed to be." He flung himself down in a chair, his long legs sprawled across the carpet, and rested a lean cheek against one sunbrowned hand.

She gave up on the idea of getting rid of him. He did this fairly often when an idea was taking shape; Katherine had long ago figured out that kicking his heels beside her desk and talking about it helped him test the usefulness of a new concept. And though Stephen's style was completely different from Rafe's habit of keeping everything to himself until he had the details worked out, in the last year she'd certainly grown accustomed to it. It was rather nice, in a way; it made her feel like a valuable part of the team.

But why did you have to pick today? she wailed silently. All she wanted right now was to be alone with her grief and her anger.

"The best part of the premiere system is its ability to call for help," Stephen said, almost as if he were beginning a lecture. "But that's also its Achilles' heel. If an intruder can stop the computer from telephoning the authorities, he can circumvent the whole system, at least for long enough to accomplish his goal." He looked at her expectantly.

Katherine sighed and played along. "Then we bury the telephone lines. Or install a dummy line, so our intruder thinks he's prevented the call by cutting the wires, but he really hasn't. Wait a minute. What about conduit? If we surround everything with metal so it can't be cut—"

Stephen was shaking his head. "You're thinking too small. Who needs lines? We can go cellular."

"As in telephone? A satellite telephone?"

"You've got it."

"Too expensive."

"We don't know that. Check on it, Katherine. It wouldn't take an elaborate telephone setup, you see— just a basic one. Also, it would be a dedicated system, used only in short bursts now and then, not to call Grandma every Saturday night, so—"

"So we might be able to get a break on the cost of access to the satellite network."

"Now you're thinking. First, let me know if it's possible, no matter what the price. Jake's working out security for an estate up in the mountains, and I want to offer him the option." He pushed his chair back and stood. "I'd also like to have some rough figures by next week on what it would cost to incorporate it into our packages. Can you do that?''

"Of course." But only if she could put aside her heartbreak and concentrate. And yet, that might be the best medicine of all. . . .

She was still writing furiously when Stephen left her office. And when he poked his head in later, she was startled to see that two hours had passed. But Irene's personal computer was hooded and her office dim, and the busy hum of the day's business had mellowed as the weekend approached.

"Do you need anything else before I go home?" Stephen asked, leaning around the door frame as if he half expected a paperweight to come flying at him. His tie was loose, he'd slung his jacket over one shoulder, and the sleeves of his white shirt were rolled up to the elbow.

Katherine shook her head. "Enjoy the play." She thought he looked a little doubtful about the possibility. "Oh, and the maître d' deserves something extra tonight. He was very helpful."

"I'll keep him in mind." He paused. "Don't work too late, all right? Rafe will have my head if he catches you here after hours."

"Then I'll have to make sure he doesn't catch me," Katherine said lightly, and turned back to her figures.

But the interruption had broken her tightly imposed self-control and allowed the pain to sweep over her again. She clenched her teeth, managing to smile, but the moment Stephen was gone she pushed her chair back from the desk and slumped down in it. She wanted with all her heart to let go and cry. But the wrenching sobs that seemed to be chasing around inside her were too threatening to release here. Someone might see, or hear, and wonder...

A tap on the door brought her upright, and another wave of agony washed over her as a lean young man with curly blond hair and an easy smile stepped across the threshold.

"Kathy? You wouldn't happen to have the proofs for the new ad campaign, would you?"

She closed her eyes against the pain. How many times he'd come in like this, she thought, always with a perfectly legitimate reason, in case someone was listening. "It's all right, Travis," she said finally. "Stephen's gone. Everybody is. You don't need an excuse to be here."

Travis Baker came across the office with a spring in his step. "As it happens, that wasn't an excuse. I really need to see those proofs. But since the coast is clear—"

He doesn't realize I know. He still believes he's managed to pull it off. She wondered just how long he thought that state of affairs could go on.

She propped her elbow on the edge of her desk and leaned her cheek against her hand, her arm forming what was almost a barricade. She made meaningless marks on the ledger sheet in front of her. "Company gossip says you've got the sales manager's post," she observed.

"It's not just gossip. Great, isn't it?" When she didn't respond, he looked at her quizzically. "I wasn't keeping it secret, Kathy. I was saving the news till I could tell you privately. What about it? Shall we celebrate tonight?"

The sour taste of bile rose in her throat. "Can't," she said, waving a hand at the papers strewn across her desk. A hateful little impulse prompted her to say,

"How about tomorrow? We could have dinner, maybe take in a show."

He shifted uneasily from one foot to the other. "I've got a business commitment, I'm afraid. I'll be tied up till late."

"If it's HomeSafe business, why not take me along?" Katherine suggested, and wondered how far she would have to push before he broke and confessed. "Now that you've got the promotion, surely we can do that. Or do you think it would be better to wait till you get settled in the job before we're seen together?"

He looked relieved. "You're so understanding, Kathy. It would be foolish to rush things now."

"I thought you might see it that way."

He frowned. "Kathy, you don't sound like yourself."

"Hurray for you." She reached blindly for another ledger sheet. "It's just as well that you don't want to take me along on your company business tomorrow, Travis, because I couldn't go, after all. I'll be at a party instead. An engagement party."

He bit his lip. "Oh."

"You took my name off the invitation list, didn't you? What reason did you give your fiancée for that? I wonder. No, don't bother to explain. I'd rather not hear it." She pushed her chair back and stood up, her hands braced on the desk. "Damn it, Travis, what kind of stupid jerk are you? Did you honestly think you could get away with it? That no one would tell me?"

"I was going to talk to you."

"And explain? Oh, I'd like to hear how you planned to do that."

"What's to explain?" he snapped. "I never promised you anything, Kathy. I sure as hell never said anything about marrying you."

He was probably telling the truth, she reflected. It had all seemed so clear at the time—so apparent they wanted the same things. Now that she thought about it, however, she realized that she'd been the one doing the planning. Travis had simply smiled. It had been an encouraging smile, or so she'd believed, but now she wondered if he had been thinking what a fool she was.

"You never said anything to discourage me," she replied sharply. "What was really going on, Travis? If Sherry lost interest in you, would you have married me after all? Is that it? I suppose you thought any connections would be better than none, so you kept leading me on, just in case you needed a backup plan."

"It isn't a crime for a man to keep his options open, Kathy."

"Is that what you call it? I call it lying, myself. So what options do you have in mind now? What do you want to be when you grow up, Travis? Vice president of customer service? Of research and development? Or are you aiming higher—Stephen's job, perhaps?"

"You'd better not try to undermine me, Kathy. Not if you like working here."

She almost laughed. "Oh, that's funny—threatening my job, when last week you were so busy safeguarding it. Somehow, I don't think it was me you were trying to protect by keeping Stephen from finding out about us, was it?"

"I suppose you're going to run to tell him?"

"Maybe I already have."

His eyes narrowed, and then he shook his head. "No. You're too cold-blooded to act on impulse—you'd make sure of the facts first."

Katherine's jaw dropped. He dared to call *her* cold-blooded?

"And before you do anything, make sure you understand all the facts," he warned. "Sherry might not be active in this company, but she's a stockholder. That gives her certain powers."

"Don't threaten me, Travis. And you might remember that Sherry's stock won't get you a job you're not qualified for, either. Being part of the family might speed your rise up the ladder, but it won't get you an extra rung."

He smiled, smugly. "That's enough. I'm impatient, I'll admit it. But I'd have gotten there someday, even if I'd settled for marrying you."

It was like a whip landing on raw flesh. "Don't worry about me," she said, very deliberately. "I'm not planning to talk. I'm too sick from embarrassment and humiliation to share my shame with anyone."

His blue eyes turned to ice. "That's the most anyone would want to share with you, Kathy."

She knew he was baiting her, and she didn't answer.

But he went straight on anyway. "You're the coldest woman I've ever known. Even Osborne has never made a move on you, has he, Kathy?"

She had to bite her lip but stayed silent.

"You're not exactly his type, of course, though I'm sure he strays from his usual path once in a while. The truth is, you're not anybody's type. Oh, you could be fun, I suppose, if you'd lighten up and stop being so damned frigid—"

"Don't sneer at my standards, Travis."

"If you had warmed up even a little, I might not have started looking around, you know. But the fact is, you never did. And you never will. Think about that when you start wondering why you aren't getting a whole lot of offers."

He gave her a long, coldly appraising look, and turned away as if he'd washed his hands of her.

Katherine kept her spine straight. Not for anything would she risk letting him see her sag into her chair. She would not allow him to see the wounds his words had made.

You're lucky, Katherine, she told herself, *you've finally seen what he's really like.* She could have married him first and then found out . . .

A little voice in the back of her brain whispered, "No, you couldn't. Because even a jerk like Travis wasn't willing to marry you, Katherine Whitman. What's wrong with you, anyway?"

She tried to drown out the voice. There was nothing wrong with her! Except for being dumb enough to believe him, to get involved with him in the first place—

And that alone, she reflected, was reason to believe there was, indeed, something seriously wrong with her.

She sat there, unwilling to move, unable to see what she could possibly do next.

The only thing she knew for certain was that the young woman who had come to work this morning, head high, confident about herself, her job, her future, her place in the world, had died this afternoon.

SHE WENT HOME eventually, mostly because there was nowhere else to go.

It was almost midnight by then, but despite the hour, the three lonely blocks she had to walk between the parking lot and her apartment building didn't bother her. She was numb; she had absorbed all the blows she could, and if a mugger would have appeared Katherine probably would have handed him her purse before he even asked for it and trudged stoically on.

But the shadows stayed in their proper places. A couple of bars along her path belched out nothing more threatening than cigarette smoke and country-and-western music. Above the dark roofs of her neighborhood, the skyline of Denver was alight. In all those brilliant buildings, people were dancing, laughing, eating, making love. Somewhere up there, in a revolving restaurant called The Pinnacle, the maître d' was probably just now presenting an obscenely large bill....

"Give it time," Katherine told herself. "Of course it's not fair. But you'll feel better tomorrow." She thought about that, and added, "Or someday."

In the apartment across the hall from her own, a voice murmured softly, and she almost knocked on the door, so deep was her longing for some human contact. But the tenants—a woman and a little girl—had just moved in a month ago, and though they'd seemed eager to be friendly, it would hardly be fair to take advantage of them. So Katherine went on into her own apartment.

It was small, but adequate—a tiny living room with a fake fireplace in the corner, a bedroom, a bath, a kitchen. As she'd told herself when she rented it, she spent so little time at home, really. Her job was demanding and her hours were often long. She seldom entertained. She didn't need more room.

And, she reminded herself coldly, she'd believed that someday soon she and Travis would be looking for a larger place, one to share.

Tonight, the apartment looked almost foreign, as if she'd wandered unknowingly into the identical building next door and gone into some stranger's home. It looked tired, too, and a bit neglected. There was a bare wall above the couch; the framed print she'd always intended to hang there remained propped in a corner. She remembered, almost guiltily, how she'd concluded that it was pointless to make the effort. It was too much trouble to find a hanger and the hammer and the measuring tape and the precise spot to drive the nail. Besides, someday soon she'd be moving. . . .

Well, *someday soon* wasn't going to come, and the quicker she faced that reality the better. Katherine flung her handbag halfway across the room and started for the kitchen to dig through the tool drawer. Only when she had the hammer out did it occur to her that one could not drive nails in an apartment at midnight. So she set it aside and sank into a chair.

Dawn found her there. She had dozed uneasily, wakening from time to time knowing that she should at least go to bed. But her intermittent dreams were bad enough as it was; to release all hold on her subconscious would be to invite worse, and so she stayed in the chair until the sun crept over the horizon, bringing the knowledge that before the day was over she must face Sherry's party.

"Why call it Sherry's party?" she asked herself bluntly. "Why not face facts and call it Travis's party? It's certainly a celebration for *him*. Or, if you must hide behind something, call it Rafe's party. He's the host—"

And Rafe was expecting her to be there tonight.

Suddenly, the apartment felt unbearably stuffy. Katherine opened the door onto the tiny balcony and took what felt like her first full breath of the last twenty-four hours.

Travis hadn't turned into a jerk overnight, she told herself. At some level, she must have known all along that something was wrong. Perhaps that explained why she'd always held back whenever he'd wanted to stay the night.

But if she *had* known, why on earth had she continued to see him? To plan to marry him? To let her life revolve around him?

Because, she reflected with painful honesty, despite what she'd just told herself, she had not, on any level, actually seen through him. The truth was that she had been taken in completely. She had been blinded by love. . . .

Maybe there *was* something seriously wrong with her. Maybe she *was* cold, as Travis had said. Perhaps it *had* been unnatural of her not to have wanted to sleep with him. After all, she'd planned to live with him. . . .

The continual, quicksand shift between blaming herself and blaming him—of not quite knowing who she was angrier at—was exhausting, and ultimately she tried to drive it out of her mind by planning various schemes of revenge.

It would be fitting, even possibly fun, to create a scene at the party tonight. Or perhaps it would be more effective just to have a quiet talk with Rafe. Or she could sabotage the sales figures somehow, making it seem that Travis wasn't the supersalesman he appeared.

Eventually, however, she concluded that plotting retaliation was a waste of time. What could she realistically do, after all? No matter how much Rafe thought of Katherine, an accusation without evidence to back it up could only cause problems. It would be her word against Travis's, and Rafe seemed to like Travis just fine, too.

She and Sherry were acquaintances, they weren't friends, and no doubt Travis had already planted the seeds of distrust in his fiancée, just in case. No, Sherry wouldn't end her engagement simply because Katherine said, "Trust me. It's the right thing to do."

Stephen would believe her, she was fairly sure of that; but her accusation wasn't sufficient cause for firing Travis. And anything short of his departure would only create more trouble in the future.

Indeed, if anyone got fired, it was likely to be herself.

She filled her day with busywork. It didn't take many projects to swallow the hours, of course, because it required a tremendous effort of will to move at all. She had to muster every ounce of energy she possessed simply to make herself choose a task and stay with it. But by dusk she had managed to hang the print over the couch, she'd dusted and straightened up the rooms, she'd even fixed herself lunch. Actually, Katherine wasn't sure if she should really take credit for that; it was only a sandwich and she'd ended up tossing all but two bites of it down the garbage disposal.

Still, she had tried, and wasn't that the important thing? If she could keep taking tiny steps like this, surely someday the hurt would be less. And eventually Travis would be only a nagging memory.

But that hoped-for time showed no sign of coming soon, and it was with reluctance that Katherine dug a party dress out of the back of her closet. It was the least favorite garment she owned, and she seldom put it on.

She chose it tonight merely because it held no memories.

At least no one could accuse her of dressing to make a scene. The dress certainly wasn't flamboyant; it was a muted shade of peach, with simple lines, a plain neck, no sleeves—minimal style. "In fact," Katherine muttered as she stared at herself in the mirror, "it wouldn't be bad at all—if I *wanted* to look like a teenage boy wearing a wig."

But that wasn't the fault of the dress, she reminded herself. Her figure looked pretty much as it had when she was fourteen—slender and basically flat. No deep-cut necklines for Katherine; she had nothing to flaunt, and she'd long ago accepted that.

She supposed that Sherry's wedding gown would be very low-cut indeed....

"Stop it!" she warned. "Don't even begin to compare yourself to her, because it will only lead to more pain."

Besides, it hadn't been Sherry's chest measurement that had attracted Travis, but the size of her stock portfolio. If she could remember that, it would help her through this evening.

Katherine was waiting in the foyer for her cab when the woman who lived in the apartment across the hall from hers came in. The little girl beside her danced along until she saw Katherine; then she stopped and stared, wide-eyed, before looking up at her mother with a gesture.

"Yes," the woman said, gesturing back. "She's very pretty." She turned to Katherine. "That must sound terribly rude, I'm afraid—"

"She's deaf," Katherine said, not taking her eyes off the child.

The woman nodded. "I try to respond verbally to whatever Alison says, so she'll associate the sign with the movement of lips. I'm sorry.…"

Katherine's heart went out to her. "Oh, please, don't apologize. I didn't realize, when I saw her before." She rummaged in her memory and turned to face the child directly. "Thank you, Alison," she said, and brushed her fingers against her lips, then extended her hand as if she was blowing a kiss.

The little girl's face lighted, and her hands began to fly in an incomprehensible silent babble.

"Oh dear," Katherine said helplessly. "That's absolutely the only sign I know. It's sort of like being dumped into the middle of China only knowing how to say 'How are you?' I'd have been better off claiming total ignorance."

The child's mother laughed. "She's going into detail about how lovely you are," she explained. "She especially likes your hair."

Katherine's fingers went to the smooth roll of glossy brown hair at the nape of her neck. She'd simply given it a twist and started jabbing hairpins in, adding a spray of flowers, not because she liked the effect, but to keep from looking as if she were in mourning or something.

"It's nice to meet you. I'm Molly Day." The woman held out her hand, only to draw it back quickly. "And since we've been in the park for the last two hours, you probably won't want to shake hands with either of us." She glanced at her palm and made a face.

Katherine laughed. "Of course I do. I hope—oh, there's my cab." She hurried out, and not until the driver asked for an address did she realize, almost with wonderment, that for a few short moments she'd forgotten Travis, Sherry, the party—and the heartbreak. In the exchange with that small child, all her normal enthusiasm had briefly flickered back to life. It gave her hope.

If I can only get through this night, she told herself, *I will be all right.*

CHAPTER THREE

RAFE'S PENTHOUSE occupied the entire top floor of one of the newest of Denver's downtown towers. Katherine had been there before, naturally, for Christmas parties and the like, but she'd never seen the place display quite the elegant patina it carried tonight.

Of course, the Christmas parties were mostly for HomeSafe's employees. Tonight, with only Sherry's friends in attendance, she'd probably brought out the really good stuff—cut crystal goblets, fine silver, delicate linens.

With a stiff bow, the butler directed Katherine toward the drawing room. She was startled by his tail-coated magnificence, and part of her desperately wanted to ask whether he had been provided by the caterer or if he was one of Sherry's new toys. But his impassive countenance didn't encourage conversation, so she straightened her shoulders and turned toward the drawing room, where the muted strains of a string quartet formed a soft counterpoint for the murmur of voices.

Get through the party, she reminded herself. That's all you have to do.

The penthouse was surrounded by a wide terrace, and on this mild July evening all the french doors had been opened to bring the outdoors in. The weather was perfect; the long, ivory silk hangings stirred in the slight breeze, and the candle flames wavered, but that was all. From her vantage point in the arched doorway between foyer and drawing room, Katherine could observe the sheen of silver, the gemlike brilliance of crystal chandeliers, and the soft luxury of deep carpets and hangings. The penthouse looked like a palace.

Katherine had always wondered why Rafe had bought it. Because of Sherry, probably; Rafe would be more comfortable in a log cabin in the woods, wearing flannel shirts and smoking his cigars in the open air, where no one could complain about the smell.

But not even the most fastidious of society matrons could have complained about Rafe's appearance tonight, she realized, spotting him across the room. His dinner clothes had been cut to perfectly fit his stocky frame, and his bushy silver hair had been given a new trim and a good brushing. Katherine was willing to bet there was a cigar hidden in his breast pocket—but at least it wasn't smoldering in his hand.

He grinned at her, stopped a waiter who was passing through with a tray, and came across the room with two glasses of champagne.

It will choke me to drink to Travis's engagement, Katherine thought. But she couldn't throw it in Rafe's face, could she? She'd just take a sip, for appearances' sake.

"Good stuff, isn't it?" Rafe said.

Katherine nodded. "Too much of this and I'll forget why I'm supposed to be here."

"Oh, I've changed my mind. You just have a good time and enjoy the party."

Katherine raised her eyebrows.

"I read the caterer's contract again," Rafe admitted. "I've already paid for a tanker load of this stuff, no matter what happens to it. Frankly, I decided I'd rather not know if the waiters are passing it out to my friends or washing dishes with it." He smiled placidly. "Sherry's in the dining room, by the way, if you want to say hello. Last time I saw Travis he was on the terrace."

"Not together?"

"Sherry's determined to surprise everybody." His gaze slid toward the entrance, where a group of guests had just appeared. "Excuse me, Katherine—duty calls."

So she hadn't succeeded in avoiding the worst moment by being late, Katherine reflected. The announcement was yet to come. It would be interesting to see how Sherry broke the news—surely it would be nothing so mundane as simply rolling out a cake in the shape of two wedding rings.

Though if the cake was decorated like a giant stock certificate...

Katherine warned herself not to be catty. That would only increase her bitterness and the chance of someone noticing how upset she was, and wondering why.

There were very few HomeSafe people, she realized. She'd be cheated of even the comfort of retreating to a corner for a business chat. And she hadn't caught so much as a glimpse of Stephen yet—but that was no surprise, when she thought about it. This was a command appearance, not the sort of party he'd really enjoy; he'd probably turn up mere minutes before the highlight of the evening.

If Stephen had been there, he would have been in the thick of things. Hilary Clayton—or whichever of her sisters-in-spirit he'd asked to accompany him—would not have been attracted to private corners of the terrace if there were people around to be impressed.

And Travis thinks I'm *cold-blooded,* she reflected.

As if the mere thought of the man had been a magical incantation, Travis appeared at the open french doors and started across the drawing room, almost directly toward Katherine.

Her breathing quickened, and she could feel the beat of blood in her eardrums. But she stood her ground; what reason was there for her to scuttle out of his way, after all? She had a right to be there. And surely he had nothing left to say to her—nothing, at least, that he would choose to say before an audience.

He didn't break step as he passed, but he watched her warily. Why had she never noticed how calculating those ice blue eyes could be?

She swapped her empty glass for a full one when a waiter came by, then wandered toward the terrace. She wasn't looking for a place to hide, exactly, but surely it was foolish to stay right in the center of things. A dim, quiet corner sounded much more inviting, given the circumstances. No one would miss her, that was sure.

She paused for just a second in the french doors. The drawing room faced northwest, and by day Rafe had a glorious and ever-changing view of the Rockies. But now, after dark on an almost moonless night, the mountain range was no more than a line of deeper shadows on the horizon.

Light spilled from the drawing room across the rough-surfaced concrete terrace, highlighting groups of people here and there. Quietly, Katherine slipped around the corner. Not as many people would come back here, on the narrower terrace outside the bedroom wing.

She leaned against the railing, her champagne glass between her hands, and looked down twenty stories to the avenue. The noise of traffic wafted up to her, muted by distance until the shriek and clatter became only a pleasant background rhythm.

The concrete barricade was cool, despite the warmth of the night. It was a solid half wall, waist high and wide enough to sit on, if anyone chose to be so foolish.

She could almost picture it—climbing onto that uncertain perch, losing one's hold, falling. The champagne flute tipped in her hands at the picture, and she clutched wildly at it. From this height, even a crystal glass, if dropped, could become a deadly missile; the thought of a human body tumbling twenty stories made her head swim so badly that for a moment she didn't know if she should pull back from the edge or just close her eyes and hold on to the railing for all she was worth.

"Katherine!" Strong hands closed on her shoulders and gave her a shake. "Are you all right?"

She looked up into a pair of concerned brown eyes. "Stupid question," Stephen muttered. "Of course you're not. Come and sit down."

Katherine shook her head. "I'm fine, really," she managed. "Just a bit dizzy. The height bothered me for a moment."

The corner of his mouth twitched a little. "Then don't stand at the edge and stare straight down," he recommended.

She had to laugh at that. It was so like Stephen—cool and matter-of-fact and straight to the point.

His hold on her shoulders loosened until it was a mere touch, not a grip to hold her upright. "Well, it is only common sense," he pointed out. "If you're nervous about hcights..."

"But I'm not. Not in general, I mean. Ski lifts don't bother me, or ladders." But then, she usually hadn't been drinking champagne when she tackled them. She looked down at the glass—she was clutching it so tightly she was surprised it hadn't smashed between her hands—and then up at Stephen again.

"You don't have to stay and guard me, you know," she said gently. "I'll be perfectly fine—really."

He let her go, his hands hovering above her shoulders for a few seconds, as if he expected her to sway again. But Katherine had one hip pressed firmly against the concrete rail to steady herself, and after a moment Stephen stepped away. Instead of leaving her there, however, he leaned against the railing beside her, palms braced flat against the rough surface, looking down at the city.

She glanced around cautiously, half expecting Hilary to burst through the french doors in search of her escort. Though, when she thought about it, she realized that Stephen couldn't have been coming from the penthouse when he saw her; she would have heard him. He must already have been sitting in the shadows when she came around the corner. And though there was a patio table nearby with several chairs drawn up invitingly, there was no sign of Hilary.

"What were you doing out here, anyway?" she asked, not that it was any of her business.

"Just thinking." He sounded almost sad.

Sad? Stephen, who never lost his sense of humor, whatever the circumstances? "About what?" she said softly. "Whoever's waiting for you inside?"

Stephen turned his head quickly and smiled a little. "No. I was thinking what a shame it is the Denver art museum looks like a storage facility for nuclear waste."

Katherine choked on a giggle. He was so incredibly, wonderfully sane—an anchor to hold on to in a crazy world. "Really? I always thought they must have got the plans mixed up with a federal prison."

"Just in case the paintings ever band together and try to escape?" His dark eyes were warm and laughing—and yet, she saw a sadness there, whatever he said.

Suddenly she couldn't bear the idea that he, too, was in pain, and she impulsively put her hand on his arm. "Really, Stephen. What's bothering you? Is it Sherry's engagement?"

He looked down at her hand as if he'd never seen one before. "Why? Do you think it should be giving me second thoughts?" His tone was curious, not challenging.

Katherine caught herself up short. Not only had the question been a bit on the personal side, but it might imply that she had reservations of her own about this engagement. She managed a casual shrug. "Sherry's very young."

"She's twenty-three." He looked at her appraisingly. "Not all that much younger than you are, Katherine."

Sherry's age was a lame excuse for her doubts; she should have known Stephen would instantly see the flaw there. She studied the dark horizon as if she were trying to memorize the vague contours of the Rockies. "Three years. And there's a lot of difference."

"You mean, you haven't been spoiled and catered to, as Sherry has been all her life."

"I didn't say that." She bit her lip and added stiffly, "I certainly have no right to comment about Sherry."

"Oh, don't apologize, I happen to agree with you. Sherry *is* immature and naive. But as she's utterly and childishly determined to have her own way, there's not much point in worrying about it, is there? Katherine—" He stopped, and then said, "I've never heard anyone call you anything but Katherine. Do they?"

Her breath froze. Only Travis, she thought miserably.

"You're shivering," he said. "Let's go in."

Katherine shook her head. "No. I'd rather stay out here." Where it was dim, and where she wouldn't have to face so many people. "My father used to call me Katie." She turned, almost surprised by her own words. "You know, I'd forgotten that."

"Forgotten it? How on earth could you forget what your father called you?"

"I was only a toddler when he died, you see." She chewed thoughtfully on a fingertip. "I don't even know if I honestly remember, or if I just recall being told. Though I'm sure my mother wouldn't have made any big deal about mentioning it."

He let the silence drag on for a moment, before saying incredulously, "Your mother wouldn't have told you things like that, to help you remember him?"

But Katherine was lost in the fog of memory, and for a moment she hardly knew he was there. "She married again," she said finally. "It—it wasn't a good second try." She looked up at him before she realized that her eyes were brimmed with tears. She turned away quickly. How stupid; just because she was hurting, she was dragging out every other old injury to study as well! "Ancient history," she murmured. "I shouldn't keep you, Stephen."

"If you're worrying about Hilary swooping out here and accusing you of trying to steal me, don't." His voice was dry.

Katherine forced herself to laugh. "She'd be very foolish to think I'd considered anything of the sort, wouldn't she?"

"Yes," he said coolly. "But at any rate, there's no reason for concern, since I didn't ask her to the party."

Katherine fumbled in her tiny bag for a handkerchief, surreptitiously removing any traces of tears. Then, try as she might, she couldn't help asking, "Why on earth not?"

He slanted a disbelieving look at her. "Use your head, Katherine. A man who invites a woman to his sister's engagement party is asking for trouble."

"I see. You think she might conclude that just because Sherry and Travis are settling down you should be starting to think the same way."

"Something like that."

She tucked the handkerchief back in her bag. "Oh, I think you're safe. Hilary isn't a fool." She wasn't looking at him.

"I certainly hope not."

An instant later the rustle of formal clothes alerted her to another presence on the terrace, just as Travis said, irritably, "So here you are—discussing business, no doubt."

Katherine shrugged. "Actually, I wasn't planning to put the last hour down on my time sheet." She turned with a saccharine smile to face him and finished off the flat champagne in her glass.

Travis's jaw tightened, but he merely said, "Sherry wants you, Stephen. It's time for the announcement."

Stephen didn't even glance at him. "We'll be along in a minute. I'm sure there will be plenty of room for us."

Travis said something under his breath and went back inside.

Katherine's voice caught in her throat. "Stephen, I'd really rather not—" She stopped herself at the last possible second. She could hardly refuse to show up for the focal point of the evening without causing comment. "I mean, I don't belong right up front," she went on, almost desperately. "I'm not family...."

"And just who said that I was planning to hover next to the happy pair? I'm going to stay on the fringes of the crowd, so I don't have to look excited for the sake of the photographs." He took her elbow, rather firmly, and guided her toward the french doors. "Come on. You have to stand somewhere."

In the dining room, Stephen disposed of her empty champagne glass and handed her a brimming one; Katherine took it meekly and cautiously looked around, trying to anticipate any trouble that might be waiting.

Next to the loaded buffet table, Sherry was standing with her father. It was the first glimpse Katherine had had of her, and her expectations were satisfied; Sherry's dress was dark magenta, with beaded trim that shimmered under the lights, and a deeply cut neckline meant to draw all eyes to her abundant curves.

I can't exactly blame her for making the most of her natural assets, Katherine thought. *If I was built like that I'd probably do the same thing.*

Rafe raised his glass, and the noise in the room died to a murmur as he started to speak. Katherine heard only a word here and there; she was concentrating on keeping her face calm, her head tipped as if she were interested.

"And now the shouting begins," Stephen murmured in her ear, as Rafe reached the end of his toast and summoned Travis from the back of the room. The young man put his arms around his intended bride and gave her an enthusiastic kiss. The crowd exploded in excited noise and rushed toward Sherry and Travis, who broke into happy grins as they were surrounded.

"We really fooled everyone, didn't we?" Sherry said, almost giggling with delight, and Travis gave her a fond pat on the cheek.

Katherine told herself that she, of all people, should not be surprised at the convincing nature of that display; after all, she had plenty of evidence of Travis's qualifications as an actor.

There was nothing she could do but to join in the toasts. At least there was one saving grace, she thought. The champagne was a very good vintage, indeed. And now that the big event of the evening was fast becoming history, surely she could just fade away.

As Sherry and Travis moved off toward the dance floor, trailed by most of the crowd, Katherine stepped out of the line of traffic, and manufactured a yawn.

Stephen looked down at her quizzically.

"I *did* work too late last night, after all," she murmured. "Sherry wouldn't notice if I just vanished, would she?"

"Sherry wouldn't notice if half the world disappeared, as long as it wasn't the half with Neiman Marcus in it." He asked bluntly, "How much champagne have you had?"

Katherine's spine stiffened. "If you're worried about me driving, you can call a cab for me. That's how I'd planned to get home, anyway."

He finished off his own champagne. "I'm going, too, now that the excitement is over. I'll take you."

She opened her mouth to refuse, and closed it again. She wasn't dragging him away from the party, that was certain, and as long as he was grasping for an excuse to escape, she might as well benefit. She shrugged. "Fine with me. Anytime a woman has an offer of a ride in a brand-new Porsche, she'd be a fool to insist on a cab."

It was several miles from the luxurious tower to Katherine's more modest neighborhood. She leaned back into the soft leather seat and watched Stephen's hands, one resting easily on the wheel, the other on the gearshift. It was a quiet ride; the Porsche's engine purred so softly she could hardly hear it, and he made no effort to start a conversation.

His silence bothered her a little, until she realized that she'd never really answered his question, and he might have reached the wrong conclusions.

"I haven't had too much to drink, you know," she said, with a hint of sulkiness in her voice. "And I didn't set out to get smashed, either. I only took a cab because I don't like walking all the way from the parking lot to my apartment after dark."

There was an empty parking spot directly in front of the building. Katherine muttered, "Great. So now I look like a liar, too." She gathered up her shawl and evening bag.

Stephen grinned at her and put the Porsche neatly into the space. He caught her surprised look and said firmly, "I'll walk you in. It's late."

She almost told him that it was nearly always late when she came home, that she was used to it and didn't need a protector. Then she looked at the dark building and thought, *I do not want to go in there alone.*

Uncomfortable as she had been at the party tonight, at least there had been some comfort in human company. She didn't want to walk into that apartment by herself, knowing another long night and another long day stretched ahead of her before she would have even the minimal solace of going back to work.

Her head was swimming a little. Perhaps Stephen was right after all, and she had drunk too much champagne. But surely three glasses wasn't enough to cause a reaction like this. Unless—suddenly she remembered the lunch she had fixed but hadn't eaten, and the laden buffet table she hadn't even touched. It would be no wonder if the alcohol was hitting her more than usual.

She let him take her key, and over the click of the dead bolt she said hesitantly, "Would you like coffee?"

She wasn't looking at him, but she could sense his surprise.

"Just coffee," she pointed out. "I mean—" She took a deep breath and tried to stop herself from turning red. She didn't want him to get the wrong idea; how perfectly embarrassing that would be!

But he said quietly, "I could use a cup," and Katherine relaxed.

He stayed in the small living room while she puttered about the kitchen, boiling water and spooning coffee into mugs. She felt vaguely dissatisfied that it was only instant, and so she rummaged around and found cheese and crackers and hard salami, and arranged them on a plate. For all she knew, Stephen hadn't felt like eating at that party, either.

He was looking at the photographs propped on the mantel when she came in with the tray and set it down on the coffee table. "Family pictures?" he asked.

She shook her head. "Mostly friends."

"That's why I didn't see a resemblance, then." He reached for a gold frame, a bit larger than most of the others. "Except for this one."

Katherine glanced at it. The photograph was a rather fuzzy representation of a young man in a military uniform. "That was my father."

"I could tell by the chin," Stephen said with what sounded like satisfaction.

"I'm surprised you can see any likeness at all. That was the best the restorers could do, considering what they had to work with." She could read the question in his eyes, and something pushed her to answer that unspoken inquiry. "I found the original in pieces in my mother's things, after she died."

"Oh, Katherine." He sank down beside her on the couch and sat there restlessly, as if ready to jump up and be off.

What a stupid thing to say, she told herself. Even Travis had never known that; why was she suddenly blurting it all out now?

You are one boring coffee companion, Katherine Whitman, she thought bitterly.

"I'm sorry," she said. "I don't normally inflict that story on my guests. It certainly doesn't matter any more." She reached for her coffee mug and turned on a smile—a meaningless, social smile that tried to say all was well and it was time for a new subject.

She might have succeeded, too, if she hadn't looked directly into his eyes and seen the empathy, the compassion, the sensitivity that lay in the brown depths. And something else, as well . . .

Her hand clenched, her fingernails cutting into her palm. "Please," she whispered.

He didn't ask what she meant; it was just as well, for she couldn't have told him. But the moment that his mouth touched hers—gently, softly, with tender understanding—she knew. This was a healing touch. This was what she needed to make her whole again....

Her hand relaxed and opened, then lifted hesitantly toward his face. Stephen's arm slipped around her shoulders and eased her back against the soft cushions of the couch.

He seemed to understand how desperately she needed to be held, caressed, desired, and he answered her plea. She didn't know how much time passed; it could have been mere moments, or forever. All she knew was that each touch, each kiss fed the next, like sticks tossed one by one onto a snapping blaze. Comfort turned to hunger, and hunger to a strange, all-enveloping desperation that ought to have frightened her—but did not.

He cupped her face between his hands and held her a little ways from him, saying in a voice she hardly recognized, "I'd better go."

"No," she whispered. "Don't."

"You know what will happen if I stay."

She wet her lips with the tip of her tongue. "I know."

He kissed her again. "You said—just coffee."

"A woman has a right to change her mind, doesn't she?"

"As long as she doesn't lose it entirely in the process."

There didn't seem to be any answer to that, so she merely pulled him down to her.

"Do you honestly understand what the hell you're doing, Katherine?" His voice had a rough edge to it, like a half-worn-out file.

"Yes!" It was a reckless lie, and she knew it, but she was past caring. Travis had said she was too cold-blooded to act on impulse, but she wasn't, after all.

And sometimes, she was beginning to understand, acting on impulse felt very good indeed. . . .

IT WAS BARELY DAWN when she woke, and she was cold. Of course, she thought muzzily; what do you expect if you throw off the covers in the middle of the night?

She reached for a blanket and came fully awake with a start. There was an arm draped across her body. A well-muscled arm, browned by the sun and hardened by tennis and racquetball and skiing. And it belonged to a man who was still sound asleep.

That was one blessing. But at the moment, it was absolutely the only one Katherine could think of.

Eyes wide, she stared at him, as he lay half-curled around her and obviously not cold at all. Color climbed faintly into her face as she remembered the madness of the night. She had been out of control, yes—but had she really made love to him like a desperate wanton?

Yes, she thought. She most certainly had. And she didn't even have the excuse of having had too much to drink; if it had been the champagne at fault, her memories would be fuzzy. But she remembered every kiss— every touch—every whisper of sensation. . . . And she would never forget how completely her desires had been fulfilled.

Katherine sank back against her pillow. *Only you could take a situation that was already messy and make it ten times worse,* she told herself. *And you thought you had problems before!*

What on earth was she going to do when Stephen woke up? When they both had to face the fact that last night she—Katherine Whitman—had efficiently, coldbloodedly, and very competently seduced her boss?

CHAPTER FOUR

STEPHEN MUTTERED something unintelligible, and Katherine's breathing froze until he was still again.

Horrible possibilities began to chase each other through her head. What if he woke right now to find her there, and in the first instant of consciousness she saw confusion in his face as he tried to remember why he was in her bed? Or worse yet, what if there was shock in his eyes—or disbelief at the memories of last night?

Or pity? That, she thought, would be the worst of all. He had felt real compassion for her when she'd told him about her father, there was no denying that. But was that the reason he had stayed with her?

He should go, he had said, but she'd practically begged him not to leave her. And he hadn't gone. Had his actions been motivated by some kind of charitable impulse—because he felt sorry for her?

The longer Katherine considered it, the less she was able to find any other reason that made sense. She wasn't—as Travis had so bluntly, rudely, but accurately pronounced—the kind of woman Stephen generally found appealing.

I think I am going to be sick, she told herself.

Stephen turned over with his back to her, and nestled his cheek into the pillow. Without the warm weight of his arm holding her fast, Katherine suddenly felt even colder. It wasn't the chill of the mountain air pouring in through the open windows and brushing her skin that was causing her discomfort, but a paralyzing cold that rose from within. What would he say when the inevitable moment came? Would he try to let her down tactfully?

With the last bit of self-control she possessed, Katherine slid over the edge of the bed. She wasn't running away, she told herself firmly. She was simply buying herself a little time to think.

She found yesterday's jeans and a cotton sweater and tiptoed out into the living room before she stopped to pull them on. The snack tray was still on the coffee table, untouched. The cheese looked dark and dry, the hard salami shriveled and curled. She left it there; what difference did it make if it aged a few hours more?

She shoved her feet into espadrilles, found her handbag and fumbled for her keys, which were not in the accustomed pocket. She lost a precious couple of minutes locating the tiny evening bag she had carried last night. Beside it on the mantel was her apartment key, where Stephen had put it. She grabbed it and turned to leave.

From the bedroom door, a husky, sleep-raveled voice said, "Hello. Or should I say goodbye?"

Katherine wheeled around.

He was wearing trousers, and not another solitary thing. He ought to have looked ridiculous, she thought, with his tousled hair, bare feet, and the formal satin-striped trousers. Instead, he looked terrific.

His mussed-up hair reminded her of how she had buried her fingers in its softness last night. Her gaze dropped as she tried not to stare. At the lean, narrow hips. At his chest, covered with soft, dark curls that did nothing to mask the ridged muscle underneath. And his face . . .

She reached for the doorknob.

"You're not going out after doughnuts, are you?" he asked, very quietly.

She wasn't certain what he meant, but the cynical edge to his voice made her quite sure that she didn't want an explanation. "Last night was enough of a mistake," she managed to say. "Please, Stephen. Don't make it worse."

"One massive mistake," he said, in a murmur she was obviously not intended to hear.

But Katherine's ears had always been keen, and that was the final blow. Fighting back a shudder, she slipped out and closed the door behind her with a click of finality. She didn't manage a full breath or a complete thought until she was three blocks away, in the parking lot, and then she slumped behind the wheel of her car and cursed herself for being such a fool.

She should have stayed and gotten it over with. She should have let him make whatever explanations he wanted, issue whatever warnings he felt were needed, no matter how badly it would have shredded the little self-esteem she had left. She would have to face him sometime; it would have been easier, in the long run, to have had it out with him this morning than to worry about what he was likely to say tomorrow, in that silent paneled office.

If she'd only had the sense to stay, it could have been settled now, and it wouldn't have seeped into their work . . .

What an idiot you are, she told herself. As if there was the slightest hope that this could remain a private matter, separate from HomeSafe! There was no way to

put this mess aside and forget it, to simply go back to
the way things had been before.

"Talk about going from the frying pan into the fire!
If you wanted to commit suicide, Katherine Whitman,
you ought to have just jumped over that railing last
night. Twenty stories straight down and it would have
been over with. This way—"

As it was, the consequences of her self-destructive
instincts were only beginning.

She drove around the city for a long time, hardly
aware of her actions. There was nowhere to go, nothing to do. And since it was Sunday, there wasn't even
work to take her mind off her problems—

Would she ever again be able to do that, she wondered. Would it be possible to bury herself in paperwork and forget everything else? Could she ever again
concentrate on HomeSafe, with this hanging over her
head?

The enjoyment of her job was shattered. The easy
working relationship she had always treasured was
gone—sacrificed in a thoughtless moment of loneliness
and despair.

She ordered breakfast at a greasy little diner in an
anonymous suburb, and pushed soggy scrambled eggs
around her plate for a while as she drank acid-strong
coffee and wondered what else she might have thrown
away last night.

She found herself wishing that she could go and talk
to Rafe Osborne. She had done that a few times before
and Rafe always listened carefully, asked thoughtful
questions and ended by giving good, solid advice. But
talking to Rafe was out of the question this time. For
one thing, she couldn't quite envision herself telling
Rafe what had happened last night. And if she did

confess, her job would be at stake. No matter how fond of her Rafe happened to be, she was an employee—and seducing the boss certainly wasn't on the list of approved behavior.

But wasn't her job even now on the line? she wondered. Stephen was every bit as adamant about proper employee conduct as Rafe had ever been. If she couldn't pull herself together soon, it would be too late. In fact, he might already have decided to get rid of her, and prevent any risk of a repetition of...

No, she told herself firmly. She bore the brunt of the responsibility for what had happened last night, but she hadn't exactly dragged him into her bedroom; Stephen was too fair-minded to blame her entirely. Still, if they could no longer work together it would be Katherine who'd be asked to leave, not Stephen.

"Time to cut the losses," Rafe used to say, when some apparently promising line of research hadn't produced the expected results. And when she'd sympathized, Rafe would only shrug. "No sense in throwing good money after bad," he'd tell her. "We'll just give something else a whirl."

Would that be his advice this time? Should she muster her courage to talk to him? Or should she wait and try to ride it out, walking a tightrope every time she saw Stephen? Perhaps the problem would fade, and eventually everything would return to normal—or to some approximation of it—if only she could keep her head long enough.

And perhaps pigs would learn to fly, too.

Maybe she should quit, while she had a chance of going with dignity and salvaging something from the experience.

Was it time to cut her losses?

She hadn't decided anything by the time she paid her bill, and it certainly wasn't a conscious decision that brought her to the guard shack at the main entrance of HomeSafe; in fact, she was almost surprised to find herself there.

"Working on Sundays, Miss Whitman?" the guard asked. "Must be an important job going on."

"Just clearing up some details, Jed." The gate opened and Katherine drove through. As long as she was here, she might as well put in a couple of hours at her desk. Getting a start on that report for Stephen on the use of cellular telephones might help; it would certainly distract her for a while and stop the wild, pointless spinning of her thoughts. By the time she was finished, she might have a better idea of what she wanted—needed—to do.

She felt a little odd, walking through the quiet building. It wasn't the empty halls and the silent labs and workrooms that bothered her; she was often at HomeSafe after most of the workers had gone for the night. But walking through in the daytime, wearing such casual clothes, felt very strange. She was usually so careful of how she looked at work.

She was well inside the executive suite before she saw that the lights were on and that someone was bent over the bottom drawer of Irene's desk. Her first thought was of the elaborate security net, and how incredible it was that anyone could have circumvented all of it and gotten in. Then the figure straightened, and her panic settled into an uncomfortable lump in the pit of her stomach.

"Stephen," she said. It was no more than a choked whisper. "I didn't expect—"

"Sorry to shock you." He closed the drawer and slapped the folder he held against the palm of his hand, as if he were trying to make up his mind about something. "But since you're here—come into my office."

It was more order than request, and automatically Katherine responded to it. As she slipped past him, Stephen made a move as if to take her arm, and she instinctively sidestepped, almost shuddering away from his touch. He stopped as abruptly as if she'd struck him.

You shouldn't have done that, she told herself. If she had only acted as she always used to... It had never bothered her before when he touched her. She'd certainly never pulled away from him as if she'd been burned.

Her instinct had been right, she thought sadly. Becoming lovers changed everything. There could be no putting this aside and ignoring it.

She bypassed the deep, comfortable chairs grouped invitingly at the end of the room and chose instead the almost straight-backed one beside his desk. Unconsciously she assumed a defensive posture—feet firmly planted on the carpet, shoulders hunched protectively...

Stephen followed her in and leaned against the corner of his desk. Katherine thought he looked almost like a bird, perching for a moment to watch for danger, with no intention of staying there for long. But the moment stretched out painfully, and neither of them moved.

Finally he broke the silence. "I'm sorry about last night. It should not have happened." His voice—even his words—was abrupt, to the point, almost flat.

It was no more than she'd expected. Katherine studied the grain along the edge of the desktop and said, "It wasn't your fault. I was out of my mind, I suppose."

She didn't look at him; she couldn't. What on earth must he think of her? What kind of woman behaved as she had last night? Did he think she pulled that sort of stunt frequently, with any man who happened to be handy? "At least, I think I must have been crazy," she muttered. "I don't—do that kind of thing."

He shifted his position restlessly. "You certainly had all the moves down last night."

She closed her eyes tightly against the prickle of tears.

Cut your losses, she told herself. You don't really have a choice; it's only a matter of time.

"I'm sorry," he said. "That was uncalled for."

Still, the harsh words had been spoken, and there was no taking their sting away. Katherine swallowed hard. "I'm leaving HomeSafe," she said huskily. "Effective immediately. I'll finish up what I can today, but I'm sure you'll understand why I'm not coming back."

He moved again, not very gracefully. "Katherine—"

She looked up at him then, eyes bright with unshed tears. "Do you really think we could work together like this?"

He didn't answer.

She stood. It took all the self-control she had to walk slowly toward the door. "I'll leave my resignation on your desk before I go, and my keys at the guard shack."

Stephen rubbed the back of his hand across his eyes. "I can't exactly give you a recommendation to take to the competition." He sounded very tired.

After all her work, after all her time and loyalty—to be refused a reference was a harsh blow. And yet, if he had written her a recommendation, Katherine knew it could only have been a guarded one, the kind that experienced personnel officers could see through in a minute. The kind she'd composed once or twice herself, at Stephen's request, when a doubtful employee left HomeSafe....

"I didn't expect that you would," she said quietly.

She made certain he was gone before she ventured out of her office to leave the carefully typed resignation letter on his desk, along with the rough draft of her report on the cellular telephones, incomplete though it was. It took just a few minutes to pack up the personal items that had collected in her office. When she left the building it wasn't yet noon.

She was putting the box in her car when she heard Travis's voice. "What's up? Stealing company secrets?"

Despite herself, her hands jerked and the box tumbled into the back of her car. She closed the trunk and turned to face him. "It's a surprise to see you here at this hour."

He grinned, breezily. "I can't say the same for you. Any normal woman who left the party with Stephen last night would still be curled up with him now. But you, of course, wouldn't even have recognized the opportunity." He paused. "Or does this mean you've decided to wait for me?"

"Wait for you to do what? Get rid of Sherry?"

"Oh, no—I wouldn't be that stupid. But after a while, I'll manage a little free time...."

"I don't doubt it," Katherine said dryly.

"Once you get loosened up, Kathy, you might be fun."

Katherine unlocked her car and got in. "Have you ever been down to Royal Gorge, Travis?" she asked politely.

"Sure. What's that got to do with—"

"Next time, jump off the suspension bridge. And don't bother with a bungee cord.'' She started the engine with a roar and backed the car out, heedless of how close the wheels might be to his toes.

There was one good thing about the situation, she told herself. She certainly didn't need to worry about Travis any more. She'd created more trouble and grief for herself than he could have caused her in a million years.

THE PHOTOCOPY MACHINE was broken, so Katherine had to walk two blocks to the nearest working model. The late August heat wave was so intense that the pavement seemed to be melting, and by the time she'd carried her stacks of paper back to the office, her once crisp salmon-colored shirtdress felt as limp as if she'd put it on two weeks ago. There was a new batch of survey forms piled haphazardly on the table in the corner beside the personal computer, and the vice president's secretary was impatiently waiting for her return.

"It's past time for my lunch break, Miss Whitman,'' she pointed out. "You might have hurried back. Mr. Cole has a client in his office with him—hold all his calls until further notice. I might add that he asked me what on earth you were doing with all your time, since those surveys don't seem to be moving. If I were you, I'd make a dent in them this afternoon or the agency is apt to get a complaint about your work.'' With a last helpful nod, she vanished down the hall.

Katherine put the stack of fresh copies on the corner of the secretary's desk and counted to ten, and then to twenty-five.

"My head aches,'' she muttered. "It's so hot it's impossible to sleep at night. I've picked up a nasty bug that I just can't shake, and it looks as if I'm doomed to enter stupid answers to a stupid survey into a stupid computer for all time. What else, dear heaven, can possibly go wrong?''

Venting her spleen made her feel a little better, except for the headache, and she sat down at the computer again with determination. However, it—like the photocopy machine and most of the other equipment she'd encountered around this office—had been a budget model, and the screen oscillated a bit, making the letters vibrate slightly and her head ache even more. She gritted her teeth and tried to increase her pace, but within twenty minutes the motion of the screen was making her feel faint and almost sick to her stomach.

She had just pushed her chair back from the desk and let her head drop forward to fight off the dizzy spell when the door of the inner office opened and Bill Cole and his client appeared.

Katherine jerked upright, so fast that the blood drained to her toes, and she would have pitched onto her face on the carpet if it hadn't been for the prompt response of Mr. Cole's client. Hands caught at her shoulders, easing her head down to her knees. "There— sit still a minute, you'll be all right," a gruff voice said.

Rafe? She tried to say it, but her voice wasn't working, and the mass of hair that had fallen over her face, along with the pressure of his hand on the back of her neck, kept her from looking up to make sure.

"What's wrong with the girl?" Mr. Cole asked querulously.

"She's obviously ill, that's what's wrong."

It was definitely Rafe, at his driest and most dangerous. Katherine knew that edge in his voice.

Rafe went on, "Does she have epilepsy or something?"

"How should I know? She's only a temporary, from one of those agencies. I don't know anything about her." The tone of Mr. Cole's voice indicated that, furthermore, he was washing his hands of this troublesome employee.

The grip at the back of her neck tightened momentarily. Katherine thought Rafe was probably unaware of his action, but she couldn't keep herself from moaning in protest.

He dropped to one knee beside her. "Are you in pain—Katherine!"

She wet her lips. "Hi, Rafe. Not pain, exactly, I'm just dizzy. And I've had flu. You know how that hangs on. I'm just not very lively yet."

"Well, you don't belong here." He helped her sit up, and kept a steadying hand on her shoulder.

"My very thought," Mr. Cole chimed in. "My secretary will call the agency and have them send someone else—someone who wants to work. I don't believe we'll be needing you in the future, Miss Whitman."

Rafe gave him a look that should have turned him into a charcoal briquette and bent over Katherine again. "Whenever you feel able to get up, I'll take you home."

"How about right now?" Her head was still throbbing from eyestrain, but she really was feeling better. And certainly some air would improve things—air uncontaminated by Bill Cole's presence.

I was just fired, she thought. Wouldn't that be the perfect finishing touch on her record? Oh, well, it was too late to worry about it now; Mr. Cole wouldn't take her back even if she begged. And if she tried to get down on her knees, she'd probably never be able to get back up.

Rafe saw the unsteadiness in her step and put his arm around her. "Damn fool shoes," he complained. "It's a wonder you women aren't all cripples. Do you have a car?"

She shook her head, and wished she hadn't. "Parking is so bad here that I've just been using the bus."

"Parking and a lot of other things—like management, I'd say. Charming sort, your Mr. Cole." He broke into song as they crossed the parking lot. "'Old Bill Cole, *not* a merry old soul...'"

"That's not tactful, Rafe." But she had to smile at his enthusiastic and off-key tenor.

"You're feeling better, if you're reminding me of my manners."

"A bit. What were you doing there, anyway? I don't remember ever hearing of any connection between HomeSafe and Bill Cole's outfit."

"And if you had, you wouldn't have been working for him, I suspect," Rafe said blandly. "I was inviting him to submit a bid for some HomeSafe components. But don't worry. He's not likely to get the job." He opened the door of his Jeep so Katherine could climb in.

"It's not exactly Cinderella's carriage, I'm afraid," he said with a sideways look at her. "If I'd known, I'd have borrowed Stephen's car. Now, tell me why the hell you were working there, Katherine Whitman." His voice was stern.

"It's only for a week or so," she said, before she remembered that she wasn't expected to return at all. "Anyway, it was supposed to last that long—this was my third day. I'm a temp for the Mayfly Agency. You know—I fill in when businesses need an extra pair of hands.''

"I know what a temp is. I just find it hard to believe that you're working as one.''

She bristled a little at the incredulity in his voice. ''It's not a bad job. Every now and then there's a Bill Cole, but most people are decent. And without a reference—'' She bit her tongue, but it was too late to stop. "It was the best I could do."

Rafe's bushy eyebrows looked fiercer than she had ever seen them before. "What in the hell happened, Katherine?''

She stared out the window and tried to pick her words carefully. He was the chairman of HomeSafe, after all; she didn't want him to misunderstand, or think she was accusing Stephen. "Stephen and I had a disagreement," she said unsteadily. "It was entirely my fault.''

"Are you telling me that he fired you? And wouldn't give you a reference?''

"Not exactly. I quit. There's my apartment house, Rafe.''

He pulled into the fire zone in front of the building without a second's hesitation. Katherine opened the door and turned to put her hand out to him. "Thank you so much for bringing me home—''

A high-pitched squeal from the sidewalk drew her attention. Alison Day burst away from her mother's grasp and came running to the Jeep. She tugged excitedly at Katherine's skirt and began making frantic gestures.

Molly, half a step behind, bodily picked up her daughter and started to carry her back to the sidewalk. Then she stopped in midstride. "Katherine! What—

you're feeling sick again, aren't you? Come along. I'll help you upstairs."

Grateful for the excuse, Katherine turned back to Rafe. "I'll be fine now. Thanks again."

But as she slid out of the Jeep, his hand closed on her arm. "Just one thing, Katherine. Stephen doesn't seem to have got the message. Your office still has your name on the door, and the official response to questions is that you're taking a leave of absence."

She was standing on the sidewalk, frowning, when he drove off.

Did he mean—could he mean—that her job was still there, if she wanted to try again? It had been more than six weeks since she'd left that letter on Stephen's desk. If he hadn't even told Rafe about it...

Alison was patting her arm. Absently, Katherine looked down to see the little girl rub her right hand over her heart.

"You're sorry?" she said. "For what, Alison?"

"For squealing like that," Molly explained. "And for interrupting. She was excited to see you, of course, but that's no excuse for bad behavior. Let's get you upstairs, Katherine. What happened, anyway?"

"I tried to faint."

"Did you succeed?"

"No." Katherine sighed. "I couldn't even finish a simple task like that and do it right."

Molly made soothing noises while she opened Katherine's door and settled her on the couch. "It's no wonder. You're so tired, dear."

"I know. I'll get over it if I can only keep going." She started to sit up, but Molly pushed her gently back against the cushions.

"Don't move."

Katherine subsided. She didn't have the energy to argue about it, that was sure.

"Did you eat breakfast this morning?"

"No. I didn't feel like it. I'm sorry to be such a nuisance, Molly. I was going to baby-sit tonight while you go to class, and here you are taking care of me instead—"

"Don't worry about it. You'll probably be feeling just fine by then."

"Is that a promise?" Katherine asked wearily.

Molly grinned, patted Katherine's shoulder, and stood up. "I'll get you some toast right now, and I'll come in to check on you later. Oh, and you might try soda crackers first thing in the morning. It sounds stupid, I know, but it really works. That's how I got through morning sickness."

She smiled briskly and headed for Katherine's kitchen. Alison pulled up a small stool, plopped down on it and began patiently asking questions one after another.

Katherine wasn't watching her. She was reeling under the worst attack of nausea, headache and dizziness that she'd ever experienced in her life.

"Morning sickness?" she managed to croak.

Molly's head appeared around the door frame. "That's what I— Oh, dear heaven, Katherine, don't tell me you didn't realize? No strain of flu produces symptoms like the ones you're having."

Katherine's voice was lifeless. "I thought maybe I was just depressed about losing my job, and that was making everything worse."

My job, she thought, and let herself remember what Rafe had said—that her name was still on her office door, and officially she was simply taking a leave of absence. He'd implied that if she wanted to walk back into HomeSafe tomorrow, she could do it. There would be questions, perhaps, and she would still have to deal with the problems that had led her to quit in the first place—but if she could put her memories behind her she might have a second chance.

A second chance. It was a beautiful phrase, full of hope.

She'd long ago admitted that she missed her job. But until Rafe had held out the possibility of returning, she'd never really allowed herself to think about how much she regretted her decision to leave HomeSafe. Since there was no going back, there was no point in dwelling on what could have been.

But she knew, now, that no matter how uncomfortable it might have been around the office for a time, it would have been better than the Mayfly Agency. She missed HomeSafe. She missed the feeling of being a valued, important part of the business. She missed Stephen, so much that she was afraid to let herself think about it....

But barely a moment after she had begun to hope, to wonder if things might work out after all if she and Stephen could only manage to ignore their one colossal mistake, the hope had been ripped away from her. It wouldn't be possible to put that night behind her and forget that it had ever happened. It would never be possible, now.

It had been six weeks and five days since Sherry Osborne's engagement party. And in slightly over seven months more—sometime around the middle of April—Katherine would be giving birth to Stephen's child, conceived on that incredible, insane night.

Hot, bitter tears flooded Katherine's eyes. She turned her head into her pillow and sobbed.

Molly perched on the edge of the couch and began to stroke Katherine's hair. "I assumed you just didn't want to discuss it," she said softly, "that you were keeping it to yourself while you considered what you want to do."

"What I want to do?" Katherine repeated, weakly, almost as if Molly was speaking some foreign language. She sighed. "I don't know, Molly. I don't know."

CHAPTER FIVE

MOLLY STAYED a while longer, murmuring reassurance, but there was really nothing she could say that would make things better, and both of them knew it. The hard choices were Katherine's to make, and it was almost a relief to her when Molly and Alison tiptoed out and left her alone.

She sank back against her pillow and closed her eyes. Her head still ached, but the rhythmic throbbing was nothing compared to the stony ache in her heart. The shock had passed, but it had left her in the lowest, most defeated mood of her life.

She hadn't known such despair was possible. But this was worse than the shattering moments in her childhood—still so clear in her mind—when she had been told she wasn't any good. This was worse than the day she'd rebelled against that abuse and left home—for then, though she was terrified at being entirely on her own, she'd known that if she worked hard enough, anything was possible. This was even worse than the day she'd walked out of HomeSafe, sacrificing the career she'd struggled to build.

But that had been the right decision after all, she reflected. Things were bad enough as it was; she would have to tell Stephen, of course, but she simply couldn't imagine herself standing beside the coffee cart some morning and announcing, as he refilled his cup, "Remember the night you stayed over at my place? Well, guess what!''

Telling Stephen would not be the average fun day at the beach, that was sure, but at least this way no one at HomeSafe would need to know. Thank heaven she'd told Rafe she had the flu. And thank heaven, as well, that she didn't have to do anything right away. She had time to consider, before she ever picked up the telephone, precisely what it was she *wanted* to do.

Which brought her back to exactly where she'd started.

She was listlessly stirring the contents of a saucepan when Molly came to check on her that evening. Molly took one look at the macaroni bubbling in the pan and the shredded cheese ready to be stirred in, and said approvingly, ''It's not exactly a balanced meal, but it's hot, and that's a start.''

''I thought Alison might like it.'' Katherine shrugged. ''Besides, it's one of my comfort foods.''

''Like Mom's chicken soup when you have a cold? I see. I can leave Alison at the child-care center if you're not up to coping with her tonight.''

''I'm fine. Actually, I'd like the distraction.''

''Well, she's certainly that. I'll remind her that you're not feeling up to playing.''

''I'm all right—physically. Emotionally, I'm a wreck. If only this wasn't happening now . . .''

''Oh, honey, I know. But think about the baby. Of course you're not thrilled with the circumstances, but it's still a miracle. A new life always is.''

''This one is more like a disaster.''

Molly's mouth tightened. After a moment, she said quietly, ''Poor child. With that kind of attitude surrounding it even in the womb . . .''

"You're right. I really am a terrible person, aren't I? I suppose if I'm going to be like that, maybe I should be thinking about having an abortion." And then she wouldn't have to face Stephen, either....

"You cannot possibly be serious." Molly's voice was crisp. "Thousands of people would give everything they possess to be able to have a baby."

Katherine sighed. "No, I don't suppose I could go through with it. Adoption, then. That's all that's left, Molly. Heaven knows I can't make ends meet now, let alone if I'm trying to raise a child." But the sudden pang of loss shooting through her was startling. Was she actually feeling the stir of maternal instinct? Surely not; it must just be Molly's talk of babies and miracles that was causing this pain. And yet, could she bear to give up her baby? Sacrifice her own child, the only human being in the world who would ever belong to her?

"What about your old job? Didn't the man who brought you home today say that it was available again?"

"Not under these circumstances—believe me." Katherine drained the macaroni and stirred in the cheese. "This will be ready in a minute, and Alison and I will let you go off early to class for a change."

Molly smiled wryly. "And get rid of the nosy friend? I'm sorry, Katherine. It's just that I know what being a single parent is like. It's not always easy, but it's not so bad, either, and I hate to see you making choices without thinking them all the way through. I care about you, honey...."

Tears crept into Katherine's eyes, and she had to bite her lip to hold them back. "You're the first person in a long time who *has* cared. I guess it's just hard for me to accept."

"That you're worth caring about?" Molly gave her a hug. "We'll have to work on that."

She turned to Alison and explained patiently where she was going, and when she would be back. "And take it easy on Katherine," she finished.

Katherine smiled a little. It had sounded more like a prayer than an instruction.

Yes, she thought, Molly certainly knew the downside of being a single mother. A profoundly deaf child would be a challenge for two parents. Katherine shivered at the idea of having to cope with such a handicap entirely alone. But was the responsibility honestly that much less if the child wasn't physically handicapped, she wondered.

As soon as her mother was gone, Alison dived into her macaroni and cheese with enthusiasm, managing to sign animatedly even with a fork in her hand. Katherine thought that Molly probably frowned on that sort of behavior, but she didn't really know how to explain to Alison that it wasn't mannerly. *Don't talk with your mouth full* didn't quite fit the circumstances. So she ignored it and tried to follow what Alison was telling her.

Despite her best efforts over the last few weeks, Katherine could still manage to catch only about one sign in three, just enough to guess at the context of Alison's conversation. Whenever the child paused, Katherine simply put her own fork down and employed the very first sign Molly had taught her. "Slow down," she said gently, and stroked the fingers of her right hand slowly over the back of the left.

Alison frowned, and heaved a gusty sigh. For a few moments she made her signs larger and more deliberate, but before long she was off at top speed again.

Katherine gave up on trying to follow, and found herself wondering just who was the handicapped one, after all. Alison's lack of hearing didn't bother the child; she didn't even seem to realize that her own way was the unusual one. Apparently she'd accepted Katherine as a slow learner whose disabilities must simply be endured.

"And you might be right," Katherine muttered.

Molly was raising a beautiful daughter. Alison was bright, happy, unspoiled. And though she was profoundly deaf, she was, in fact, less handicapped than many children Katherine had run into—children who didn't know the limits of discipline, or the sunshine of love.

"I wonder if I could do as well," she said to herself.

"What?" Alison signed politely. "Repeat?"

"Never mind. Would you like ice cream?" Her pidgin signing obviously got the point across, for Alison nodded eagerly, carried her plate over to the sink, then patiently waited beside the refrigerator with her spoon until Katherine got the carton out. And before she took her dish back to the table, the child gave her a bear hug, as if to say that she understood and sympathized with Katherine's disabilities, and liked her in spite of them.

The gesture touched Katherine's heart. Some things were the same in all languages, she thought. The unselfconscious hug of a child...

For the first time she found herself thinking of the baby not as an interference in her life, but as a person-in-waiting. Boy or girl, she wondered. With Stephen's dark eyes, or her own hazel ones, or something in between? More important, would this child be as happy as

Alison was, or as haunted as Katherine herself had been?

She wandered into the living room and picked up the picture of her father, wondering if someday in her child's face she would see something of him—and if she would be able to recognize it. She searched the blurred image intently, finally putting the picture aside with a sigh. It was hard to make out what he had really looked like. The original had been so small, so faded, and so heavily damaged that the reproduction, poor as it was, was something of a miracle.

Katherine had never known whether her mother had torn up the original in a fit of rage and then regretted her action, or if her stepfather had been the one who destroyed it.

It didn't matter, she supposed, except as a lesson. The baby she carried would never suffer that way. She would make certain of it. No matter what she had to do...

She sat there for a long time, watching as Alison played with a fashion doll, and considered her next move. She was so absorbed that she jumped six inches when the telephone rang. Alison, of course, didn't even twitch in response.

"Katherine?" Rafe's voice was gruff. "I thought I should check on you. Are you still holding together?"

She shifted her grip on the telephone and dried her suddenly damp palms on the seat of her jeans. "Of course. It's very kind of you to call."

"Well, I'm glad you're feeling better. Listen, I'll be talking to Stephen tomorrow. If you want me to ask him about that job of yours—"

"No, please," she said, too hastily. There was a suspicious silence on the other end of the line. "Rafe, please don't say anything to him about me."

"Katherine, don't be silly."

"I'm not. But it will be better if I talk to him myself. I'll call him soon, Rafe—I promise."

There was a brief pause. "You're certain you're feeling better?"

"Absolutely. I'm fine, Rafe."

At least, she would be eventually, she told herself. She would work things out somehow—just as she always had before.

ARMED WITH MOLLY'S all-purpose soda crackers, Katherine was able to work the rest of the week, though the Mayfly Agency agreed that she shouldn't go back to Bill Cole's office.

On Saturday she managed to get to the supermarket, the laundry, and the pharmacy, and was bemused to find that everywhere she went she saw babies—in strollers and in backpacks, in ones and twos and even threes. Were there suddenly more of them, she found herself wondering, or had she simply never noticed before?

In the afternoon she wandered down the block to the ice-cream shop to buy a sundae, then carried it across the street to the park to watch the children play. It wasn't the first time this week that she'd gone there, to sit and watch and ask herself questions as if she were preparing for some sort of test.

What if she was the mother of the toddler in the sandbox who had just bonked his playmate over the head with a truck; how would she handle it? *Could* she handle it? Or what if hers was the injured child? Would she react correctly? How did a mother know whether to kiss the wound or rush the child to the emergency room, anyway? And what about the sand—or mud, or snow?

Did she honestly have the patience to sit here accomplishing nothing while her child played, and enough stamina left over to clean up the mess afterward?

Because it's not just a baby you need to think about, she reminded herself. It was a person—a toddler, a child, an adolescent, a teenager—for whom she would be taking responsibility. And if she couldn't handle that challenge, with only herself to rely on, then she had better admit it before long—while there was still time to arrange an alternative.

The thought of adoption left her cold. Had she made a decision, then, without even realizing it?

A shadow fell across the bench and she automatically moved to one end to leave a place for the newcomer.

"You told Rafe you were going to call me," Stephen said.

Every muscle in her body tensed. It took an effort of will to turn her head to look at him.

He looked different, she thought. Perhaps it was the casual clothes—jeans and an open-neck Polo shirt that left his arms almost bare. Or was it simply that she'd never seen him without at least a glint of humor in his eyes before?

She finished the last bite of her ice cream and set the plastic container beside her on the bench. "And I meant that. I just didn't say when," she said coolly. "How did you know where I was, anyway?"

He shifted his weight, propping his elbow on the back of the bench, and looked out across the park. His eyes were hidden behind the dark lenses of his sunglasses, but she could see the fine lines at the corners of them, deeper now than she remembered—or was it only that the sunlight was so strong?

"I ran into your next-door neighbor," he said. "Don't blame her—she was very cautious. She looked me over for a full five minutes before concluding that I was probably not a serial killer."

Even without his usual executive garb, Stephen could convince anyone to trust him, Katherine thought. It really wouldn't be fair of her to blame Molly for not holding out. "So she sent you here?"

"To be precise, she said you'd gone to the park to play your own masochistic version of Let's Pretend. Whatever that means."

Katherine smiled despite herself. Molly thought she was crazy even to be considering the question of whether she would be a good and capable mother. Of course she would, Molly had announced, and now would Katherine kindly get on with more important matters, like deciding how she was going to manage everything. The idea of adoption Molly refused to discuss at all.

Katherine frowned. Had Molly sensed her decision, before it had even been made?

"How are you feeling?" Stephen asked. "Rafe told me you haven't been well, and I can see it for myself." His fingertip went out as if to touch the hollow in her cheek, and then dropped away before it brushed her skin.

She could see herself reflected in the shiny dark lenses of his glasses—her face thinner, her hair caught up in a careless knot at the top of her head, her eyes shadowed. "I'm feeling fine," she said, and steeled herself for what had to follow. But she couldn't look at him while she said it, so she picked out a small boy on the lawn and watched him toddle uncertainly across the grass while she added, in an undertone, "For a pregnant lady, that is."

She didn't know what she had expected—that he would shriek and jump up and run off across the park, perhaps, or go wild-eyed and start tearing out his hair by the handful—but she'd underestimated his style. The president of a major corporation doesn't show surprise, she reminded herself, no matter what the calamity.

And if, despite that code of self-control, Stephen's jaw had tightened a fraction or his mouth had shown the merest hint of distaste—well, that was the main reason she hadn't been looking at him as she broke the news. If that was what he felt, she didn't want to know it just now.

His voice was quiet. "Have you seen a doctor?"

"Not really. But I managed a quick visit to a clinic. There is, unfortunately, no chance that it's only my imagination."

"Have you thought about—options?"

She looked at him, but trying to read the expression behind the dark lenses was fruitless, and she couldn't see even a hint of what he might be feeling.

I was wrong, she thought. *Any expression—any emotion—would be better than indifference.* She found herself wanting to kick him in the kneecap just to see if that might break his calm.

"You know, Stephen," she said earnestly, "sometimes you'd be a lot more likable if you'd react like a human being instead of a chief executive officer. What the hell do you mean, have I thought about options? I haven't thought of another damned thing in the last three days!"

He rubbed his knuckles along his jaw. The action made Katherine feel better; at least it was some sign that he might actually be agitated. "What have you decided?"

The little boy she'd been watching toddled uncertainly over to a woman sitting on the grass. His wet, toothy smile showed his obvious pride in his new skill, and his mother enfolded him in her arms with apparent joy.

I want that, Katherine thought. *And telling myself that I can accept anything else is just another version of Let's Pretend.*

Making the decision didn't take the fear away. But there was a little nugget of peace in her heart as she admitted how strongly she'd already come to feel about the baby.

"I can't give up my child," she whispered. "I can't live with wondering if he's all right, if he's happy, if someday he'll hate me for giving him away. I couldn't stand wondering if, accidentally, I gave him up to parents like mine were. So I'll keep him safe in my heart, and I'll do the best I can to love him and provide for him—" Her voice broke. "Oh, dammit, I don't want to cry, but I always planned it to be so different! I wanted a pink-and-blue nursery in a house in the suburbs for my baby—"

And a dog, and a sandbox and a little brother or sister. And most of all, a father who would arrive home at the end of the day, eager to see the child who waited patiently for him to come—

Well, all that was out of her reach, wasn't it? So she might as well accept what was, and do the best she could.

She fumbled for her paper napkin and blew her nose. "Stephen, will you give me a reference so at least I can get a decent job again?"

He was obviously startled; his arm jerked against the rough back of the bench and he swore. "That's what you want? A job?"

"I'm certainly not asking for a handout." She couldn't look at him. "I take full responsibility for this."

"Money wasn't quite what I had in mind."

His voice was very quiet, and her brows drew together in puzzlement as she turned to study him. "Then—what do you mean? What are you suggesting I do?"

He leaned forward with his elbows propped against his knees, and looked directly into her eyes. "What people have always done when there's an unexpected baby on the way, Katherine. They get married."

As soon as her dizzy spell passed, Katherine leaned back against the hard slats of the bench, fanned herself with the newspaper Stephen had dug out of the nearest trash container, and said, "What are you, anyway? Temporarily insane? You don't want to get married."

For just an instant he looked as if he were about to nod in agreement, but he said, mildly, "That's beside the point. This changes lots of things."

"Not necessarily. Having a baby is a terrible reason to get married, Stephen."

"Is it really?"

"Yes. You don't want to marry me any more than I want to marry you."

"Nevertheless, you're going to have to be practical, Katherine. You know bloody well you can't make it on your own."

"Yes, I can. If you'll give me a reference—"

He said, almost brutally, "You could go to work for the competition any day, without one. They'd love to have you—and what you know about HomeSafe."

"I wouldn't do that to you, Stephen."

"Well, you'd better learn to give up your scruples fast, because unless you're selling HomeSafe secrets, you can't make enough money to support yourself and a child. You're good, Katherine, but jobs of the caliber you're used to don't turn up in every corporation. And even if they do, they require total dedication. How in hell do you expect to work sixteen-hour days if you're coping with a baby?"

She hadn't considered that. "Then I'll get a job I can handle."

"It won't pay enough. Katherine, don't you understand that you'll have to let me help?"

She turned her wristwatch round and round, and said wistfully, "I could come back to work for you. If my hours could be just a trifle more flexible . . ."

His voice was gentle. "You aren't thinking very clearly, are you? Can't you imagine the consequences? The questions?"

She could. Her bottom lip was quivering a little.

His hands, warm and strong, came to rest on her wrists. "Do you know what it costs just to have a baby, Katherine? I don't mean raise it and send it to college, I'm just talking about the medical expenses before the kid is six weeks old. Pink-and-blue nurseries don't come cheap—"

"Don't laugh at me, Stephen! I have a right to my dreams!" Her voice was muffled; she pulled her hand away and bit her knuckle to keep from crumbling into tears again.

"Of course you have a right to dream," he said softly. "You have every right to want the best for this baby." He brushed a loose tendril of hair behind her ear. His fingers were trembling. "That's what I want, too, don't you see?"

She swallowed hard and tried to blow her nose again. There wasn't a dry patch left on her paper napkin. Stephen dug a handkerchief out of his pocket and handed it to her. It was soft and pristine white, and it smelled like him—like spice and musk and summertime.

"There's nothing abnormal about having only one parent these days," she said stubbornly.

"Maybe there isn't," he conceded. "But are you willing to tell him someday that you settled for that—when he could have had more?"

"That's not fair, Stephen." There was a tinge of warning in her tone.

He pressed on anyway. "He can have the pink-and-blue nursery in the suburbs, and everything that goes with it."

For a long, tempting moment, she allowed herself to consider his offer. Was it fair to her child to turn it down? It wasn't the idea of lacy cribs and elephant-decked wallpaper that was the real lure, of course, but everything else Stephen was implying: private schools and violin lessons and ballet shoes and all the things that she would never be able to afford on her own, no matter how hard she tried.

She knew her temptation showed, and she steeled her heart. "Material things aren't as valuable as a parent's love," she insisted, but her voice sounded hollow.

"It's hardly a case of giving up one to get the other. Quite the contrary, in fact."

He was right. If she accepted this offer, her child would have Stephen's concern, his caring, as well as hers. The love of two parents. Exactly what she had told herself a few minutes ago that she wanted—or, at any rate, almost exactly that. If he actually wanted to know his child...

He can't, she thought. He's only feeling sorry for me.

Stephen was watching the struggle written in her face. "You wouldn't have to hold a job at all, if you didn't feel like it," he said quietly.

"It's the quality of the time that counts for a child, not the quantity."

"I don't think you really believe that. And in any case, what kind of quality time can it be if you're exhausted, worried and overworked?"

"That's my problem, not yours." She swallowed hard. "I don't want to ruin your life, Stephen."

"Dammit, would you stop being holier-than-thou for one minute?" He sounded furious, and it startled her; she tried to pull away. Stephen cupped her hands between his, and said very gently, "There really is only one question left, you know. It's the only one that matters."

She frowned uncertainly.

"What is best for the baby? If you truly want what's best for the baby, Katherine—"

She swallowed the lump in her throat. "All right," she whispered. "I'll think about it. And you should, too. No hard feelings if you change your mind." Before he could answer, she freed her hands and pushed herself up from the bench. "I'll let you know next week, Stephen."

"No." He glanced at his wristwatch. "Go home and have a nap. I'll pick you up at seven for dinner. We'll decide it tonight."

She stared at him. "But that's only two hours. I need some time to think about this."

"No, you don't." His voice was firm. "Time won't make it any easier to decide, because two days or two months won't make the facts any different, Katherine."

And she couldn't argue about that, could she?

HE TOOK HER to a sleepy little restaurant in Denver's oldest hotel, where business was very quiet. She wasn't surprised that he hadn't chosen The Pinnacle; there, they might run into anyone from Hilary Clayton on down, and she was certain Stephen would much rather avoid the questions that would bring.

Still, if she did what he was suggesting, questions would be inevitable, and the possibility that he was uncomfortable about facing them made her a bit uneasy. Some small imp of annoyance made her say, "I didn't know this was one of your usual haunts, Stephen."

He outmaneuvered the maître d' and held her chair himself. "I considered The Pinnacle," he said, "but I thought a revolving restaurant might make you feel seasick. Besides, the tables here are far enough apart to allow truly private conversation."

It was a perfectly reasonable answer, and Katherine's gaze dropped in embarrassment to the pale pink napkin the maître d' had just spread across her lap. Of course he didn't want to create interest before they'd even decided what to do!

"Shall I send the wine steward over, Mr. Osborne?" the maître d' asked, and looked surprised when Stephen declined.

"Not tonight. I think we'll have some sparkling water, instead. Any particular kind, Katherine?"

She shook her head. "You needn't try so very hard to take care of me," she murmured.

Stephen gave her an appraising look. "It appears to me as if somebody needs to do a better job of it."

She stared down at her menu. It was completely illogical to take that comment as a put-down. He knew she hadn't been well, and when a person was ill, it was a great comfort to have someone helping out.

So why did she feel that what he was really saying was that she looked awful?

It wasn't fair, she thought. She had taken great pains to appear at her best tonight. She was wearing her favorite dress, of a deep red fabric that made her eyes look darker and threw reflected color onto her cheeks. She had also done her best to cover up the dark circles under her eyes—at any rate, if those shadows were what he was talking about, he shouldn't blame her for their existence. Take a nap, indeed! Had he really expected her to go blithely off to sleep with everything she had on her mind this afternoon?

The wine steward brought them a bottle of sparkling water, opened it and poured it, managing all the while to maintain an air of disapproval over his customers' plebeian tastes.

Stephen lifted his glass. "Shall we have a toast?"

"To what?"

"To the baby. To the future."

Katherine left her glass sitting precisely where the wine steward had placed it. "Stephen, I just don't know..."

Stephen sighed and set his glass down.

"What you've suggested is a pretty drastic solution to a problem."

He shrugged. "It's a pretty drastic problem. And what's so crazy about my solution?"

"Why marriage? All right, I admit I probably can't make it on my own. I'll probably need some financial help. But—"

He frowned at the bubbles in his glass. "If I'm going to be the financial support for this, I think I should have a say in the rules. Don't you?"

She looked at him. "It will cause a lot of talk, you know. The man who was never going to limit his options, suddenly turning up with not only a wife but a baby—"

"So maybe I started listening to Rafe. He's certainly been telling me for long enough that a wife would be an advantage. Maybe he's right. I admit it's not the romantic match of the season, but—"

"You can say that again," Katherine muttered. She wondered if he realized that he was nervously toying with his flatware in a way that Emily Post would never have approved.

He didn't seem to hear her. "—getting married is not the end of the world, either. And it's the only thing I can think of that solves all the problems." He gave his soup spoon a push and realigned his fork. "This way you can even have your job again, if you want it."

She blinked a little. "You really do want me back?" she said, uncertainly. "I thought—"

"Want you?" Stephen's smile glinted in the candle-light. He leaned across the table to take her hand and said, "All right, you've caught me. I admit it. I'm only doing this because the piles of paper are threatening to bury me. I can't live without you, Katherine. I'll do anything to get you to come back to HomeSafe."

She tried to pull her hand away; he held onto it. "Working well together is not exactly a good foundation for a marriage," she protested.

The teasing note died out of his voice. "It's not a bad one, either. Who knows what we might be able to build on it?"

She closed her eyes and whispered, "What do you want from this marriage, Stephen?"

He hesitated, and when he finally spoke his voice was level and matter-of-fact—and she knew he meant every syllable. "I want this child to be safe and secure and cared for. That's all."

She looked down at their linked hands resting on the linen cloth and thought, *We liked each other enough to get into this mess. Perhaps he's right in thinking that we can build something together. Something for our baby...*

"All right." Her voice was very soft. "I'll try."

His was truly a beautiful smile, she acknowledged. Reflections of the candlelight danced in his eyes, and what seemed to be a wave of warmth swirled around her, comforting her and soothing her doubts.

And it was a beautiful thing he was doing, as well. She knew that many men, under similar circumstances, would have questioned, hesitated, perhaps denied responsibility altogether. Many more would have had to be pushed into giving even minimal aid to the child. But not Stephen....

So why should she suddenly feel suspicious? Why did she have a nagging feeling that Stephen was following some hidden agenda—a script she couldn't comprehend or even see?

Why did she feel as if, when she wasn't looking, she'd been turned into a marionette—with an invisible someone pulling the strings?

Don't be silly, she told herself. No one had the power to manipulate. her. And no one would even think of trying.

CHAPTER SIX

THE CAR AHEAD of Katherine's passed through the security gate into the HomeSafe complex, and she took her foot off the brake, letting her car ease up to the guard shack. "Hello, Jed," she said pleasantly. "New uniform?"

The security guard grinned and looked admiringly at his dark blue coat sleeve. "Right—everybody's got them. Aren't they nice? Mr. Osborne said you'd be along to ask for your keys." He leaned out of the shack to drop them in her hand, and Katherine went on through the gate.

It felt strange to be there. It seemed almost as if nothing had changed—that the last seven weeks had been only a crazy dream, and that this was like any other Monday morning at HomeSafe. And yet, little things *were* different. Jed's new uniform, the fact that there was a car occupying the parking spot she had habitually used—and those things formed a nagging reminder of what a strange turn her life had taken.

She was very late, and the hallways of the office wing were already bustling. That, too, was a reminder of how different things were now. She had always been one of the first to get to work.

Inside the executive suite, Irene looked up with a smile. "Boy, am I glad you're back. How was the vacation? Did you go somewhere exotic?"

To Katherine's relief, the door of Stephen's office opened. He stopped on the threshold and stayed very still for a moment, looking at her with something in his eyes.... Concern, of course.

He had called her on Sunday, to check on how she was feeling. But she hadn't seen him since Saturday night when he'd taken her home after dinner. Suddenly, she felt almost shy under that intense gaze. She tried to cover her discomfort by studying the paisley pattern of his tie instead of looking at his face.

Stephen gave what sounded almost like a sigh of relief. "I was worried about you." His voice had a husky edge.

Aware that Irene was listening with interest, Katherine said carefully, "I got a slow start this morning, that's all."

His eyes lit with understanding. "Come on in. Irene, call the lab and tell them I'll be a couple of minutes late." He ushered Katherine into his office, his hand merely brushing her arm, and tossed his leather notebook on his desk.

Rafe would approve of the desk, Katherine thought. It was no longer pristine and uncluttered. She eyed the haphazard stacks of papers and folders littering the office. "Well, I can see what I'll be doing all week," she muttered. "Funny—I hadn't heard about a hurricane hitting Denver, but obviously it came through here."

Stephen gave her a rueful smile. "It's not as bad as it looks, really," he protested. "And I didn't bring you in here to dump a load of work on you. I just wanted to tell you that the wedding will be Wednesday afternoon."

Her hand clenched on the report she'd picked up. "Wednesday?" she said blankly. "Do you mean the day after tomorrow?"

"Yes. That's really the earliest it can be managed. Just a small ceremony, in the chambers of a judge who happens to be a friend of Rafe's. I hope that's all right?"

She nodded. "Yes, of course. But—"

"You'll need to go down to the company clinic this morning and have a blood sample drawn, by the way."

"But Wednesday, that's so soon. Won't Rafe think it's a bit odd?" Her hazel eyes were wide with worry. "Unless—you didn't tell him about the baby, did you, Stephen?"

There was a momentary silence. Then, very gently, Stephen said, "It's not going to be any big secret for long, Katherine."

"But to be in such a rush . . ."

"The middle of April will be here before you know it, and people can count."

She was silent. She could feel her cheeks growing red with embarrassment, not only for herself but for him as well.

Stephen had turned back to his desk, to take something from a bottom drawer. It was a flat square package, a couple of inches thick, wrapped in glossy silver paper. He handed it to her. "I thought you might like this."

She took it reluctantly, but it obviously wasn't jewelry or masses of flowers. She'd feel even more of a counterfeit if he was to present her with things like that, and she was grateful that he was sensitive enough to realize it.

She cautiously pulled the paper back and opened the box. Under a thick layer of tissue was a square white volume, its leather cover smooth and plain . . .

No, not plain, she realized. Down in the corner, in gold type, was a name. Baby Osborne.

She couldn't read the bits of type on the vellum pages because of the tears in her eyes. She clutched the book to her breast and put one hand to her face.

He's being so damned decent about everything, she thought, trying to swallow a sob. He deserves better than this. . . .

Stephen's index fingertip stroked the upswept curve of hair above her ear, so gently that she scarcely felt his touch. "Look, don't worry about it," he said softly. "People will talk. There's no way around it. But by the time we get back, they'll have most of the gossip out of the way and we can all get on with life."

"By the time we get back?" Katherine repeated unsteadily. "Where are we going?"

"I thought we'd spend a few days at Winter Park, at the condo."

A honeymoon. At a ski resort that didn't even have snow at this time of year! A twinge of pain shot through her as she realized how different things should have been—planning her wedding trip, the first few days alone with her new husband.

"At this season, it's practically deserted up there," Stephen said. "I thought perhaps it would be better than—" He stopped abruptly.

Of course, Katherine nodded, following his reasoning. Better the condo, quiet and private and isolated, than some honeymoon resort where everyone would expect them to behave like all the other newlyweds.

"But if you'd prefer something else, Katherine . . ."

She'd always dreamed of a lazy honeymoon full of
sun and sand and tides—Hawaii, or Bermuda, or Ja-
maica, or the south of France.... But those dreams
would only hurt her now, so she pushed them away and
shook her head. "No, the condo will be fine. I'll make
the arrangements." She turned her attention back to the
stack of papers. "Would you like me to go through
these here, or take them to my office?"

There was a note in his voice that sounded like relief,
as if he was happy to have the subject changed. "Stay
here if you like. I'll be in the lab all morning."

She looked up from a balance sheet. "Do you need
me there?"

"Well, yes, I'd like to have your impressions. But are
you sure it's safe for you? The noise..."

"Stephen, I'm pregnant, not handicapped," she said
crisply. "I can still do everything I did before." She put
the report down.

He smiled. "All right. This paperwork has been here
for a while, already. It can wait a little longer."

The moment they reached the lab, however, Katherine began wishing that she'd hidden out in her office
instead. The big room was buzzing with talk, and there
were far more observers than usual. "What are we testing, anyway?" she murmured to Stephen. "Defense for
the White House?"

Across the room she saw Rafe, cigar in hand, wandering around the set and studying the installation.
Anticipation trickled uncomfortably down her spine.
She hadn't expected him to be there; he so seldom
showed up for product testing. And she had absolutely
no idea what he might do or say when he saw her.

*Why didn't I ask Stephen precisely what his father's
reaction was?* she asked herself. He'd said the judge was

a friend of Rafe's, but did that mean Rafe had made the arrangements for the ceremony? And if he had, did that imply approval, or merely unwilling acceptance?

Rafe liked her; he'd always liked her. Even if he wasn't thrilled about the upcoming wedding, he surely wouldn't make a scene—would he?

Yes, she thought. He would, if he felt like it. She'd seen it happen dozens of times.

The moment Rafe saw her, his scrub brush eyebrows soared, and he excused himself from the sales representative he'd been talking to and made his way across the room toward Katherine. It took an excruciating amount of time for him to get through the crowd, and when he finally came up to her Katherine's body was so rigid that she could have doubled for the bronze statue in the lobby.

Rafe's eyebrows had drawn together in what was almost a scowl. "So you're going to marry my son, is that it?"

The question was like a rock dropped in a pond; shocked silence spread out in ripples across the room and all around them people turned to hear the answer.

Katherine braced herself for worse to follow, but instead of continuing the attack, Rafe grinned and gave her an awkward hug. "Welcome to the family, Katherine."

She stopped holding her breath, releasing it with a soft whoosh.

Rafe heard. He held her off a little and added, "Did you think I was going to forbid the banns or something?"

No, Katherine thought. *Not exactly. But I'm still not certain that you wouldn't like to.*

For there was something behind the smile that she didn't quite understand, and a shadow in his eyes that looked suspiciously like doubt—or distrust—or misgivings.

And who could blame him for that?

IT WAS, as Stephen had promised, a very small group of people who gathered in the judge's chambers for a brief and unpretentious ceremony late on Wednesday afternoon. Molly fussed over Katherine's plain nutmeg-colored suit, muttered about her lack of veil or ornament, and glowed when Stephen turned up with a nosegay of chrysanthemums and daisies for his bride. Jake Holland was Stephen's best man; he kept nervously checking his pockets and moving Katherine's ring from one to another. Rafe and Sherry came in together; to Katherine's surprise and relief Travis wasn't with them. Before she had a chance to think about whether she should ask about him, the judge came in, and it was time.

During the ceremony Alison, taking advantage of her mother's distraction, wormed her way to the front of the room, turned around to face the action, and leaned against the judge with her nose almost buried in Katherine's flowers. From the corner of her eye, Katherine could see mortification rising in Molly's face as her daughter craned her neck to stare up at bride and groom, entirely oblivious to the silent lecture she was getting from the sidelines.

Katherine wasn't mortified; she was having a hard time keeping her face straight. Her only concern was what Stephen might think of this solemn little person who was studying them both so critically. When she turned to face him in order to repeat her vows, and saw that the corner of his mouth was twitching and his eyes were alight with unholy enjoyment of the situation, she almost burst into giggles. She managed to control herself, but her voice was warm with laughter as she pledged herself to him. His voice was low, intense. Katherine wasn't surprised; of course he was feeling solemn, under the circumstances.

Afterwards, the guests gathered around them. Sherry brushed cool lips against Katherine's cheek and murmured congratulations. "Who would have thought Stephen would make it to the altar before I did?" she said. "Of course, if you're content to have no frills whatsoever, I suppose it doesn't take long."

Beside her, Jake slapped Stephen on the back. "Well, I guess I don't have to worry any more about Hilary Clayton setting traps for you, right?"

Katherine didn't think she wanted to hear the answer to that. "Have you chosen your wedding date, Sherry?" she asked, rather desperately.

"June, of course." With distaste, Sherry glanced down at Alison, who was tugging at Katherine's hand. "There will be no children at my wedding. Travis and I feel they don't belong at solemn occasions."

If that was a warning, Katherine thought, it was an unnecessary one. In June, her baby would be two months old, and the mere idea of a child that age crying throughout an elaborate ceremony sent shudders down her spine. She tried to keep her voice casual. "Where is Travis, by the way?"

Sherry shrugged irritably. "Business. Isn't that what it always is? He's been gone more in the last few weeks than he's been here."

"It will quiet down when he gets settled in his new job, no doubt."

"It had better," Sherry muttered.

Jake Holland seized Katherine for a bear hug. "Keep an eye on that ring," he warned. "I've been guarding it with my life, so don't you let it vanish." He grinned and gave her a warm kiss on the cheek. "And take good care of my buddy, you hear? You're a lucky girl. It isn't just any woman he'd tie himself down for."

Katherine's good humor vanished in one of the sudden, blinding changes of mood that she was quickly becoming accustomed to.

He isn't doing it for me, Jake, she thought. *And he'd rather not be doing it at all.*

THE AFTERNOON was fading as they drove over Berthoud Pass, and by the time they reached Winter Park dusk was settling in earnest. Light still sparkled on the ski slopes, but it seemed to Katherine that in the depths of some of these narrow mountain valleys, the sunlight never struck at all, much less stayed around long enough to warm things up.

She had been to Winter Park, of course; it was within easy range of Denver, so she'd often gone out for a day of skiing. But she'd never been there in the off-season before. Even though Stephen had told her it was very quiet at this time of year, she was a bit surprised to see that in the fall, Winter Park was a sleepy little mountain town with every third business closed up altogether.

It would begin to stir, he said, as November closed in. By Thanksgiving, the snow machines would be running and the slopes would be open, and at Christmas the place would be wall-to-wall people.

He sounded as if he found that prospect less than inviting, and Katherine was wondering about it as the

Porsche turned into a long private drive that curved around the base of the mountain.

She'd never seen the Osborne condo, but she knew it was in the most elite of Winter Park's many resort developments. The service for people who owned units there, or rented them for a week or two, was said to be superb, and Katherine had always found the staff to be perfectly pleasant when she'd called to make arrangements for Stephen's weekends—

She gasped and clapped her hand to her mouth.

Stephen jammed on the brakes. "What's the matter?"

"I forgot to call and tell the manager we were coming."

"That's all? From your reaction I figured there must be a ten-ton truck bearing down on us, at the least."

"Did I shriek? I'm sorry. But what if they've rented the place out for the weekend?"

"Who do you think would want it, this time of year?"

Katherine shrugged. "I don't know. Somebody who doesn't ski and can't afford the rates during the season, maybe."

"I suppose you're right. But it's not for rent."

"Ever?"

He shook his head. "It's bad enough trying to avoid Sherry's parties at the best of times, without coordinating schedules with the reservations desk."

"I thought that was part of the deal—when the owner isn't using the place, it can be rented."

"A lot of people do that, yes. It helps with the expenses. But it's a bloody nuisance because you can't leave valuables lying around, and you have to make an appointment to stay in your own place."

She shook her head a little. "Then why do you always call to let them know you're coming?"

"That's just so there will be food in the refrigerator."

"Oh. They take care of grocery shopping, too?"

"When asked." There was a smile in his voice.

Katherine wasn't so easy on herself. "No food," she muttered. "Well, that's just great. Some personal assistant I am. I think my brain's gone soft."

He reached over to muss her hair. "What's the matter, Katie? Are you hungry?"

Katherine sighed. "I'm generally hungry these days," she admitted. "Until I see something edible, and then all urge to eat promptly goes away."

"Well, don't worry. Not everything in Winter Park closes in September." He stopped the car at the main entrance and left the engine running. "I'd better go in and let them know we're here, so no one reports us as burglars."

"Good idea," Katherine said, but he was already gone. The air that had swirled into the car was colder than she'd expected, and she edged her feet closer to warmth from the heater. At this elevation, winter always came earlier than it did down in Denver, and from the feel of the air, this year it was just around the corner.

Stephen was soon back, and in a couple of minutes he was ushering her up a covered ramp on the side of the building with the best mountain view. He set down their luggage and unlocked the door, a cedar-covered slab so rough that Katherine hoped she never had to push on it with her bare hands.

"I think the style is called rustic contemporary," Stephen said, noting her expression. "I believe the architect chose it because it's too rugged for teenagers to carve their initials in.'' He left the luggage sitting in the hallway and started turning on lights.

Katherine followed, trying to look around discreetly and not stare. This place was *huge*—as big as the average house, and a whole lot nicer. And everything was so sleek and modern and well put together...

Stephen caught her eyeing a closed door and said, ''Go ahead and explore. But there's one thing I want you to know—''

His tone set off warning bells in her head.

''Anything embarrassing that you might happen to find belongs to Sherry.''

Katherine managed to smile. ''That's certainly a nice blanket statement.'' She sounded faintly cynical, just as she had intended. He didn't need to pretend that he was some kind of saint.

But there seemed to be nothing out of place. She glanced into the bedroom wing and counted three rooms, each with its own attached bath. There was a big living room with deeply cushioned couches and a field-stone fireplace that occupied most of one wall. There was a small terrace that looked out over a wildly wooded hillside, creating the illusion that the condo sat alone in an untouched landscape. The dining area could seat twelve with ease, and the kitchen—well, it took Katherine's breath away.

It was open and airy and efficient, with a breakfast bar along one side, an electric barbecue grill built into the range, an elaborate microwave, and a row of cabinets that might hide any number of exciting things. ''This is wonderful,'' she said, and poked her head into the refrigerator. It was empty, of course, except for a row of seasonings and sauces. ''I have this sudden urge to tie on an apron and start kneading bread or something."

Stephen pulled a stool up to the breakfast bar. "The manager promised to call in a grocery order first thing tomorrow."

"Not till then?"

He smiled at the woebegone look on her face. "We won't starve, Katherine—there are restaurants. Unless you'd rather have pizza delivered."

"I'd rather have a steak, and cook it myself." She caught the sulky sound of her voice and smiled ruefully. "Sorry. I don't have temper tantrums often, I promise. What kind of restaurants do we have to choose from?"

He folded his arms on the edge of the breakfast bar. "You're serious, aren't you? About wanting to cook?"

She nodded. "It would be like playing house. This is nicer than any kitchen I've ever had."

He smiled slowly. "Get your coat, we'll go buy a steak. And heaven help you if you char it. You might not be eating much these days, but I'm starved."

They ended up in the next town before they found a supermarket open, and from the instant they walked inside, Katherine should have realized what would happen. But she was absently assembling her mental shopping list—a nice sirloin, two big potatoes for baking, a carton of sour cream, a head of lettuce—and so she didn't notice that Stephen had disappeared until he returned with a cart.

"We don't need that," she said.

He shrugged. "It will be easier than juggling things."

They were only halfway down the first aisle when she realized that shopping with Alison—or, for that matter, any five assorted preschoolers—was probably nothing compared to the challenge of shopping with Stephen Osborne. If he saw something he liked, he put it in the cart.

Besides the steak, he tossed in chops and chicken breasts and half a ham. "For sandwiches," he told Katherine earnestly. "In case we want to go on a picnic."

Then he added a carton of eggs, a bag of apples, huge slabs of two kinds of cheese, a gallon container of popcorn...

Katherine protested when he took a three-pound can of coffee off the shelf. "Just how long are we planning to stay, Stephen?"

"Oh, through Monday or so. Why?"

"You couldn't consume this much coffee by Monday if you ate the grounds raw."

He shrugged and put it in the cart. "So, we'll leave the rest for next time. How about herbal tea? Do you like that stuff? And raisins—it's always nice to have raisins on hand."

"Stephen, this is ridiculous."

"It's in case you start craving things."

"I don't think it's me you're worried about," Katherine muttered.

He flashed a smile. "You're at least partly right," he admitted. "I don't want to drive up here in the middle of the night when you get a longing for peanuts or something." He snapped his fingers. "I almost forgot the peanuts."

"I don't like peanuts," she said firmly.

"That's all right. I do, and we can feed the rest to the chipmunks." He wandered off to look for the nut section.

Katherine sighed and pushed the cart on down the aisle. She found herself in the middle of the infant section, studying rows of baby foods and juices and cereals. There was also a well-stocked section of toys, aimed at the tourist traffic, she supposed. She noticed a particularly adorable stuffed elephant, wearing a floppy bow tie with Winter Park printed on it. Katherine picked it up. She had never seen a stuffed animal with quite so much personality....

Stephen took the elephant out of her hand and inspected it with raised eyebrows.

"I thought it would be perfect for the nursery," Katherine said diffidently. "I think I've got enough cash to buy it. I wouldn't expect—"

He dropped a casual kiss on the tip of her nose and carefully put the elephant in the cart with his bag of peanuts. "That's what the household account is for," he said cheerfully. "Necessities like elephants and ice cream...how did I manage to forget the ice cream?" He headed for the freezer cases.

"Now I know why you have the manager stock the place," Katherine muttered as she watched the grand total appear on the checkout monitor. "It's less expensive."

"Not really. He knows what I like." Stephen wrote out a check and handed it over to the clerk, then flourished the leather folder at Katherine. "Don't let me forget to put your name on the household account."

"Only if you promise to let me shop by myself."

"Why?" He sounded injured. "I didn't object to the elephant."

"Because I'll take what's left over, invest it in the stock market and get rich."

He let her carry one small bag up the stairs, but he brought the rest up himself. The steak was already scenting the whole kitchen by the time he'd unpacked their purchases. "You weren't kidding about wanting to knead bread, were you?" he asked when he found the packets of yeast she'd included. "Three of them? Talk about me overbuying . . ."

She took the package from his hand. "It's the smallest size they make. Go and build a fire."

"Yes, Kate," he said solemnly.

She was smiling as she turned back to the lettuce she was tearing into bite-size pieces. It startled her when she realized how much at ease she felt, and she wondered if that had been the purpose of Stephen's joking around at the supermarket—to break the ice and make them both more comfortable, to let them pretend for a while that they really were just playing house instead of entering into this solemn, scary contract. To get them through the evening, at least—

And after that? What happened after that?

They'd never talked about what came next, or about the extent of intimacy they would share. She'd avoided even thinking about that; it had seemed silly, somehow, to worry about it, considering their reason for getting married. And yet . . . tonight . . .

Stephen was lying on the hearth rug when she brought their dinner into the living room. For a moment she thought he was asleep; then she saw that he was staring into the crackling flames.

"Thinking heavy thoughts?" she asked, before it occurred to her that perhaps she didn't want to be told what was occupying his mind. She hurried on, "One steak. Definitely not charred."

Stephen sat up. "We do have a real table and chairs."

"I know." She put the plates down on the coffee table and settled herself cross-legged on the carpet. "I didn't want to miss out on the fire."

"Then I'll take care of the mess afterward, and you may lie here and luxuriate in the warmth." He cut his steak, sampled it, and nodded approvingly.

Katherine managed to eat half her dinner, then lay beside the fire while he cleaned up the kitchen. She was lulled almost to sleep by the soft irregular crackle of the embers as she watched the red flames reflected in the glass fireplace doors, in the high polish of the coffee table, in the stones that lined her wedding ring.

It was the first chance she had had to really look at the ring; she'd never seen it before this afternoon when Jake, after a moment's panic about which pocket he had ultimately stored it in, had handed it to Stephen. It was a wide gold band, very simple, with a deep groove etched all the way round. In the groove was a row of baguette diamonds, set so close together that they looked almost like a single endless stone. It was classic; it was simple; it was perfect.

She yawned, and found herself wondering sleepily if Stephen had realized that an elaborate engagement ring would have made her uncomfortable. Probably he hadn't given the matter any thought at all, other than to decide that a three-day long engagement didn't really need a ring to be official.

The kitchen lights went off, leaving the fire and a couple of dim lamps as the only source of illumination. Stephen came into the living room and quietly dropped to the floor beside her.

Katherine deliberately kept her breathing even and steady.

Stephen's fingers stroked the silky length of a loose lock of hair. "It's late," he said. "A good night's sleep will make you feel much better."

In a different tone of voice, it might have sounded like a prelude to seduction. As it was, it was plain and matter-of-fact and logical. *Go to bed,* he was saying. *Nothing else is going to happen here.*

It was thoughtful of him, she told herself. He was very sensitive to understand what a strain all of this had been.

But there was a little lump of confusion in the precise center of her chest.

She sat up slowly. "I am tired," she said. She hardly recognized her own voice.

He rose, of course, and helped her to her feet. "I put your bag in the back bedroom," he said. "It's the quietest—not that there's much noise here at this time of year."

She remembered the room. It overlooked the terrace and the wooded hillside. And it held twin beds.

"I'll be across the hall from you," Stephen added. "Call me if you need anything. Otherwise I won't disturb you. Sleep well."

It was only then that Katherine realized that despite her earlier misgivings, her uneasiness, her apprehension, the one thing she had never anticipated was this flat rejection. She had not expected to be sent off to bed like a child—on her wedding night.

She managed to mutter, "Good night," but she wasn't sure if he heard her. He was poking at the fire, turning the remaining logs and adding a new one, when she left the room.

Her bag was already laid out at the foot of one of the twin beds. She tugged at the straps; her fingers were shaking.

"You can't say you weren't warned," she told herself. "You just weren't listening very well."

I want this child to be safe and secure and cared for, Stephen had said. That was all. He'd said nothing about Katherine, nothing about the two of them, except in connection with the baby. How could she have been so stupid as to have let herself forget for a moment what all this was about?

She unpacked her robe and slippers, telling herself that she was glad he was such a perfect gentleman. She was grateful that he was so thoughtful of her comfort, and so understanding of her state of exhaustion.

But she was not glad. She was not grateful.

Instead she felt shunned and rejected, and more alone than she had ever felt in her life.

CHAPTER SEVEN

MOLLY MUST HAVE MADE her coffee awfully strong this morning, Katherine thought. The scent had not only seeped across the hall and through her apartment, it had even permeated Katherine's pillow. She lifted her face, sniffed deeply and appreciatively, and turned over so she could truly savor the smell. In a little while, she'd get up and make some for herself....

"Wake up, lazybones."

The sound of a male voice in her bedroom brought her fully awake, aware that she wasn't in her apartment after all and that it wasn't Molly's coffee she was smelling. She opened her eyes to a rather hazy view of a bright yellow mug—hazy because the mug was suspended less than two inches from her nose, and to properly focus on it would have required her to cross her eyes.

Behind the mug was a moss green sweater. Stephen was sitting on the edge of her mattress. "Well, now I know that an automatic coffeemaker plugged in next to your bed works better than an alarm clock. I thought you were never going to wake up."

"You said to sleep well," Katherine reminded him. She stretched and started to push herself up from the pillow.

"I didn't say to sleep all day. It's halfway to noon. No, don't sit up—dry toast first." He reached for a plate on the bedside table and popped a bite-size piece in her mouth.

"Who ordered that?" Katherine said, through the crumbs. "Molly?"

Stephen shook his head. "A friend of mine who's an obstetrician. If you don't have a preference for a doctor, by the way—"

"I don't."

"Then I'd like you to see Julie."

A woman? Well, that wasn't any big surprise, Katherine reflected. He had a lot of female friends, and most of them were high-powered in one way or another. "Is she good?"

"Well, I don't know from firsthand experience, you understand," he drawled, "but I've been told that she's very good indeed." He took a long pull from the mug.

Katherine looked at it longingly. "Isn't that my coffee you're drinking?"

"Eat your toast and I'll get you some that's hot—the way this was when I first brought it in."

She obeyed, and he vanished for a bit. While he was out of sight, Katherine punched at her pillow and ran her fingers through her hair. She couldn't tell what it looked like, but it felt as tangled as a ball of yarn after a whole litter of kittens had chased it around the house. She was wearing no makeup, of course, and her mouth felt as if the army had marched through.

It didn't matter, she told herself stoutly. He'd seen her at her worst—sound asleep, face smashed against a pillow, probably snoring. She couldn't hope to repair that sort of impression, no matter what she did to herself.

Not that it would make any difference. He'd made it entirely too plain last night that any attraction she'd ever held for him had been the fleeting sort.

He came back with a second mug, bright blue this time. Katherine sat up cautiously and reached for it.

Stephen perched on the side of the other twin bed. "Feeling all right?"

"I'm not marathon material, but I'm better than usual. I must look a fright."

His gaze moved slowly over her face. What was he doing, she wondered. Counting her freckles?

"Yes, you're feeling better," he said, and reached out to tuck the blanket around her.

Katherine hadn't realized until then that it had slipped. Not that it mattered, really; she was wearing an ordinary old flannel nightshirt, not some sexy negligee. Still, she felt a bit uncomfortable all of a sudden about making a display of herself. "I'd better get up," she said quickly. "I shouldn't keep you sitting here all day."

"Take your time. Julie said to stay still for half an hour before you stand up." He rose. "I'm going down to the lobby to get a newspaper."

The door clicked shut behind him, and Katherine lay back against her pillows, aggravated at herself. She faced half an hour of lying in bed, with nothing to do or think about, and like a fool she'd practically told Stephen to leave. She could at least have had company. Not that she blamed him for going; what an utter, boring nuisance she was. And they were facing days of this—

"I want to go home," she said.

The sound of her words, small and hopeless, reminded her that there really was no home left to go to; the movers would be packing up her things by now, under Molly's watchful eyes. She was committed. She had chosen this course of her own free will; she couldn't even accuse Stephen of misleading her.

So the only thing she *could* do was make an honest effort—as she had promised yesterday in the judge's chambers. She'd made a vow to do her best to make this marriage work. Presenting a cheerful face and not complaining certainly couldn't hurt. They had agreed to try to build something between them for the sake of their child. If the most they could manage was friendship—well, compared to what some couples ended up with, that wasn't such a bad deal, was it?

She reinforced her decision with a pep talk in the shower, greeting Stephen with a genuine smile when she reached the kitchen. "Anyone for a walk?"

He laid his newspaper aside. "Are you sure?"

"Well, I'm not prepared for a hike straight up the mountain. But if you know where there's a flat trail..."

He grinned. "Yes, I do. Relatively speaking, of course."

The trail was not flat, but they meandered up and down through the pine trees at a gentle pace, and Katherine found the exercise and the crisp air stimulating. When they came back, she tackled her lunch with gusto.

Stephen, watching with raised eyebrows as she demolished her salad and sandwich, said, "Same time tomorrow?" and Katherine nodded.

They made a habit of it after that, and over the next few days they explored a number of trails. Sometimes they packed a picnic, once they rented bicycles, but usually they simply strolled along. They talked of the scenery, or of business—there were enough safe subjects, Katherine found, that it was relatively easy to stay away from the threatening ones.

On the last walk of their long weekend, almost at dusk on Monday evening, Katherine was climbing over a fallen tree when her foot slipped on a patch of frost. She grabbed for support, arms flailing, and lunged into Stephen.

He had just crossed the log himself and was turning to help her down when she fell. He staggered a little as he unexpectedly took her weight full against his body, but he managed to keep his footing. Katherine clutched at him, eyes shut tight, feeling dizzy and expecting any moment to feel the harsh scrape of pine bark, for it seemed impossible that she had fallen clear of the log.

Instead, all she felt was the scratch of wool against her cheek, and when she finally dared open her eyes, it was to see the muted tweed of Stephen's jacket in almost microscopic detail. She moved her head just enough that her nose was no longer smashed into his collarbone and closed her eyes again. It was warm here in his arms. She hadn't realized until now how chilly the evening had become. And she was a bit short of breath, too, from the shock as well as the exertion, so she might as well be comfortable while she got her second wind.

His fingertips felt chilly as they slid under the mass of glossy brown hair to rest at the nape of her neck. And his lips were cold—but comforting, nonetheless—against her temple.

Katherine sighed and turned her face a little.

Stephen chuckled. "Playing possum, are you?" he said huskily. "A little more of that, and I'll think you engineered that fall on purpose."

Stung by the accusation, she pulled back, and realized that she was standing squarely on the toe of his boot. Remorse swept over her and she hastily stepped aside. "I've hurt you, haven't I, landing on you like this?"

"If something had to be ground into the gravel, better my foot than your face." He sank down onto the fallen tree, raising his foot and twisting it experimentally.

Katherine stood still. "Now you're lame."

"It's all right, I'm sure, just a little bruised."

Katherine went straight on. "I suppose we can build a fire to hold the grizzly bears off for a while, but eventually it won't matter anymore. We'll starve to death out here in the wilderness, won't we?"

Stephen put his foot down and tested his weight. "Hardly. We're only a hundred yards from civilization. The resort is right around that corner."

Katherine heaved an enormous sigh. "Have you no spirit of adventure, Stephen Osborne? I was just getting fired up for a fit of melodramatic hysterics in order to take your mind off the pain in your foot."

"Next time, if you'd like, I'll sneak up behind you and do my imitation of a howling wolf."

"That would certainly make it easier to have hysterics."

"What happened to your enthusiasm for the wilderness?" He grinned at her and reached for her hand.

It wasn't the first time they'd held hands as they walked along, but somehow in the dusk, on their last night in Winter Park, it just seemed natural for their fingers to be interlocked, sharing warmth and strength.

And Katherine found herself wondering what would have happened back there beside the fallen tree if she had said, "Yes, Stephen. You're quite right. I engineered that fall on purpose."

But she hadn't, of course, so it would have been a lie to say she had.

SHE'D LEFT THE terrace door open when she went out, and she could hear the soft rustling from inside the condo as Stephen gathered up another armload of possessions to take down to the car.

It was early; the valley was light, but the sun had not yet made its appearance above the line of mountaintops. She'd set her alarm clock last night, and when Stephen brought in her coffee and toast this morning she'd already had the half hour of still meditation that his doctor friend recommended. It seemed to help; Katherine found herself looking forward to meeting Julie and finding out if she had any other magic formulas.

Stephen had been surprised to find her already awake, and he was obviously worried that she hadn't slept well. Katherine had shrugged off his concern. This way, they could be back in Denver with most of the morning still ahead. He'd smiled at her eagerness and gone off to finish packing.

But the truth was, she was no longer as anxious to get back to the city as she once had been.

A chipmunk came out of his burrow just yards from the terrace. Only his rapid, jerky movements drew Katherine's eyes to him; when he was still, his striped coat camouflaged him until he almost disappeared against the rocky soil. She tossed a couple of peanuts in his direction. He watched the nuts land and warily made his way over, nose twitching, to survey the gift.

"See?" Stephen said from the terrace door. "I told you we'd use up the peanuts. In fact, we don't have much food left at all, except for the yeast."

Katherine wrinkled her nose in mock annoyance. "It takes time to bake bread, you know. If you hadn't kept me outside for hours every day—"

He flicked her cheek with his hand. "I'm glad I did, because you look better than you did last week. You've got some color in your face now."

She was obscurely pleased that he'd noticed—and it wasn't just her imagination that the image in her mirror looked healthier these days. "It must be the frostbite." She shivered dramatically.

"I think you've got that backward, doesn't frostbite make you paler? Everything's in the car. Are you ready to go?"

Her hands tightened on the steel rail of the terrace. *No,* she thought. *I'm not ready. Despite everything, we've actually started to be friends, but when we return to the real world...*

But there was no choice, so she nodded and dropped the last handful of peanuts over the rail to become a feast for the small striped animal, and she turned her back on Winter Park.

They got caught in the morning rush hour on Denver's west side and traffic slowed to little more than a crawl, but still the time flew too fast for Katherine's comfort. She deliberately steered the talk to business, feeling that it might make the transition easier, and she didn't notice that they had missed the freeway exit leading to the HomeSafe offices until they were well past it.

"I thought you'd like to get settled at home first," he said, when she asked him where they were going. "The movers should have delivered your things by now, and as the housekeeper's there today, she can help you unpack."

His apartment was in a tower not far from Rafe's. The building was older and slightly less luxurious, and the apartment itself wasn't as large as she'd expected. To her surprise, it wasn't much bigger than her own small place had been, and it was far tinier than the condo in Winter Park. It looked almost cramped with the wall of boxes that the movers had stacked in the foyer.

"I see what you mean about getting settled," Katherine muttered. "I didn't realize I had so much stuff." She looked around in growing dismay. Obviously Stephen already had everything he needed, and there simply wasn't room for more. "What on earth am I going to do with it all?"

"If you aren't going to want it right away, call the building supervisor. He'll put it in the storage room downstairs with your furniture."

"Oh, dear, I'd forgotten about the furniture." She looked around unhappily. If she couldn't have any of her own possessions out she'd feel like a guest in a hotel somewhere. Yet it wouldn't be fair to displace Stephen's things, and there simply wasn't room for both. "Stacking it in a storage room isn't exactly a long-term solution. It might be better if I bought a big garbage can."

"Don't be in such a hurry. We'll be looking for a house soon anyway, and you'll want your things then."

It was a perfectly sensible plan, and it should have delighted her. But Katherine found herself swallowing hard at his matter-of-fact tone. She had upended Stephen's life, and he was taking it so calmly that it made her nervous.

"I'll go find Mrs. Atkins," he said, and started down the hallway.

Katherine stood her ground. "Stephen, what I said about a house in the suburbs and a pink-and-blue nursery wasn't a demand, you know."

He stopped in the doorway. "Of course it wasn't. But we really don't have a choice. This place only has two bedrooms." He vanished toward the back of the apartment.

And with the baby, they would need three. Obviously, Stephen was quite content with things just as they were.

Katherine folded her arms on top of the nearest stack of boxes. Her fingers clutched at her forearms until her knuckles were white with the strain.

This was a mistake, she told herself. Why had she ever agreed to this? She should have known it would only make more trouble in the end. What was she, anyway—some kind of shrinking violet, afraid to be on her own? Why hadn't she realized that one dreadful blunder couldn't be wiped out by making a second one?

A tear dropped onto the surface of the uppermost box and turned black as it struck the ink left by her felt-tipped marker. Valuable, she had written across the top of it. Handle with Care.

She ripped the tape off the box with her nails and rummaged until she found the most precious thing she owned. It was silly to think that having it in her hands would make any difference, but somehow right now there was comfort in holding her father's picture.

She cradled it between her hands. The glass was smudged with fingerprints, so she breathed on the surface and rubbed it clean with her handkerchief.

Stephen came back in so quietly that she didn't hear him at first. "Katherine, this is Mrs. Atkins, who takes care of the place. Mrs. Atkins—" He looked over

Katherine's shoulder at the picture she held and said, "You're crying. Was that damaged in the move?"

"No. Not at all. It's just a bit dirty, that's all." She finished polishing the glass and set the frame aside. "There. That's better."

"You've put the original somewhere safe, haven't you?"

"It's in here, at the moment." She gestured at the box.

"Why haven't you put it in the vault at HomeSafe?"

"Because I never thought of that." She flipped through the contents of the box and took out a small, plain white envelope. "Will you do it for me?" The envelope fluttered out of her hand, floating to the floor, and she picked it up, automatically checking the contents to be sure nothing had escaped. It had been a very small photograph. Now it was only a dozen slivers of paper.

Stephen tucked the envelope into the breast pocket of his blazer. "I'd better get out of your way, hadn't I?"

His mouth brushed Katherine's softly, and he was gone.

She pressed her fingertip against her lips. *Don't fool yourself*, she thought. *That was a demonstration for Mrs. Atkins's benefit—nothing more.*

KATHERINE LIKED Stephen's obstetrician friend on sight, and her first examination confirmed the intuition. Julie Quinn was quietly efficient, but she managed to leave the impression of having all the time in the world if a patient should need it. And though she was a young woman, she had a comforting air about her that reminded Katherine of what grandmothers were supposed to be like.

After she'd finished the exam, the doctor took Katherine back to her office. "I've got a diet for you to follow, of course, and an exercise plan, but it's basically common sense. No alcohol, avoid caffeine, stay away from smokers—" She pushed the office door open. "Hello, Stephen. I'm not surprised to see you here."

He put a magazine aside. "I stopped in to see Katherine, and your office staff didn't want me contaminating the waiting room."

"The truth is that he couldn't wait for you to give him the results," Julie said to Katherine, without bothering to lower her voice. "You know how the bossy sort operates. Everything's fine, Stephen. There are no apparent problems and no risk factors, so we're expecting a perfectly normal pregnancy and a healthy baby. Somewhere between April second and the sixth, if you want to plan to take the week off. I'm sure your child wouldn't dare be anything but punctual." She gave him a mischievous grin and turned to the filing cabinet behind her desk. "Here's the basic information you'll need, Katherine, and I'll see you in about a month. If you have any doubts or problems, call me—anytime."

"I like her," Katherine said as they left the clinic. "Very much. Thanks, Stephen."

"My pleasure." He sounded a bit preoccupied. "I'm going out to the plant in Boulder."

She tried to summon up a mental picture of his calendar, and could only remember vague entries. "I think you've got appointments this afternoon."

"I'll be back by then." He walked her to her car. "I'm glad everything's all right, Katherine."

She sat behind the wheel of her car for a couple of minutes, telling herself that it was unfair to be disappointed by a muted response. What had she hoped for, anyway—a passionate embrace in the parking lot? It wasn't as if there had been any reason to think there was a problem—so why should there be a celebration when things turned out as expected? Wasn't it enough that he had broken up the morning's business to come to the doctor's office? She ought to be pleased by that, at least—

She might as well be honest with herself. If he hadn't been on his way to Boulder, he probably wouldn't have come at all.

It was fortunate, she reflected, that things were so busy at HomeSafe these days. She had too much time to think, as it was.

RAFE WAS OCCUPYING his favorite spot in her office when she returned. His feet, in worn-out sneakers, were propped on the corner of her desk, and the ever-present cigar, unlit, was in his hand. In his jeans and pullover shirt, he looked like a handyman, and she would swear there was grease lodged under his fingernails, as if he'd been tearing apart a car engine in the parking lot.

"Well?" he demanded as soon as she came in. "How's the little one?"

It was the first time he'd admitted to knowing about her pregnancy. The directness of the question, and the fact that Rafe had sounded as if he was gritting his teeth as he asked it, sent shivers up Katherine's spine. She didn't answer; she walked around her desk, sat down and said, "You aren't very happy about the baby, are you, Rafe?"

His gaze dropped to the cigar between his fingers. "It's not the way I'd have planned it, no. But that's beside the point. Kids get a certain age, they do what they please. Sometimes they make mistakes."

"Rafe, I'm sorry."

He didn't seem to hear. "Take Sherry, now—miserable, and won't admit it."

What a dear he was, Katherine thought, making a valiant attempt to cover up his slip by turning the conversation to Sherry!

"I ruined that girl, Katherine. Now she expects to be able to shop her way through life." He chewed thoughtfully on the cigar. "I've got some advice for you, by the way. Or maybe it's more like a favor. I don't know."

Katherine braced herself.

"You make sure Stephen is there when the baby's born. Don't let him miss out, and regret it."

His words touched her heart. "Is that the voice of experience, Rafe?"

"It certainly is. I was there when both my kids were born. That wasn't quite the thing to do in those days. The doctors didn't know how to cope with me. But they survived the shock. Take my word, Katherine—it's very important for both of you. And for the baby, of course."

There was a tap on the door.

Rafe let his feet drop to the carpet with a thud. "I'll get out of your way," he said. "Maybe I'll wander down to engineering and offer them the advantage of my experience." He gave her a slightly crooked grin.

As Rafe went out, Diane, the sales representative, came in. "Travis sent me up to ask about the brochure on the new system. When is it going to be back from the printers?"

"Not till next week, but I've got a mock-up here." Katherine turned to the credenza behind her desk to look for it.

Diane was watching the glitter of diamonds on Katherine's left hand. "I knew it didn't make sense."

"What? The new brochure?"

"No. The fact that you denied all attraction to Stephen. Nobody could work with him for a year and not feel that magnetism of his. I should have known something was in the wind. And now—it's like a Cinderella story, isn't it?"

Not quite, Katherine almost said. She found the mock-up and passed it across the desk. She was glad Travis hadn't come for it himself, but something made her ask after him anyway. "Are things so busy down there that Travis can't get out of his office?"

Diane rolled her eyes. "Out of it? He's hardly ever in it. He seems to be trying to visit every sales rep west of the Mississippi in the shortest possible time."

Katherine remembered that Sherry had said something of the sort at the wedding. "He's off inspiring his new troops, perhaps. If he succeeds, we might all get a bonus at the end of the fiscal year."

Diane snorted and eyed Katherine's wedding ring. "Some of us need it more than others, of course."

As Diane left the office, Katherine reached for her coffee cup, realized it was empty, and made a mental note to ask Irene to buy some decaffeinated. She wasn't going to be successful at following Julie Quinn's suggestion and eliminating coffee from her diet altogether, not if she kept working.

The hormone imbalances of early pregnancy caused strange reactions, she mused. Like this sudden self-centeredness. It was almost funny, but right now decaffeinated coffee was of far more concern to her than whether Travis Baker made a success of his new job or not.

SHE'D ONLY BEEN BACK from lunch for a short while when Stephen came in, and his afternoon appointment, a supplier of the hard plastic cases that protected HomeSafe's sensors, was already waiting. But before he met with the man, Stephen poked his head into Katherine's office. "I'll be tied up for awhile," he said. "Is there anything going on that I need to know about?"

"Jake was in and wants to talk to you. Nothing critical."

"I'll call him as soon as I'm free. When Irene gets back, would you ask her to make reservations for two at The Pinnacle for tonight?"

She was startled, and then she remembered that the supplier was from out of town. "Of course. What time?"

"Early. Seven should be okay."

She made a note.

"You're writing things down now?" he asked curiously.

"After the fiasco over groceries at the condo? My brain seems to have ceased functioning when it comes to food."

"Nonsense, our shopping expedition turned out just fine."

"I know—all except for the yeast."

Stephen grinned. "I wasn't going to mention that."

"Oh, and here's the report on the system we were testing last week." She handed it to him.

Stephen flipped the pages idly. "You've finished it already?"

Katherine shrugged. "You were anxious to get the results."

"I thought I told you to take things easy."

"I'm being careful."

She grinned as he studied the stack of papers on the corner of her desk. Less than a week back at work, and she'd managed to make a considerable dent in the mess that had cluttered his office. His eyes narrowed. "Did you have lunch?"

"Yes," she said sweetly. "Jake took me to Jolly's. Would you like me to file a report on what I ate?"

The corner of his mouth twitched in the prelude to a smile. "No. But when you have time, Katherine, check into putting a day-care center somewhere in the plant."

Katherine stared at him. "Why?"

"Because if we have a day-care center, maybe you'll come back to work after the baby's born. It's obvious I can't do without you." He collected the supplier and vanished into his office.

Katherine put her pen down and rubbed her temples. It was nice to be appreciated, she thought. Even if it was only her work that seemed to get his approval. So why didn't she feel happier?

Perhaps she simply needed a break. She could take off a bit early tonight and see the new show at the art museum. If Stephen was going to be occupied with a business dinner anyway, he certainly wouldn't miss her.

She worked steadily for the better part of an hour, then went to get a snack from the machines down the hall; when she came back she was startled to see Hilary Clayton sitting in Irene's office.

It was just like the old days. Every blond hair on the woman's head was precisely in place. The blue of her designer dress made her huge eyes look like still water. And her gaze was as cool—and as dismissing, when she glanced at Katherine and then turned away—as it had ever been before.

If the woman was an ice-cream cone she wouldn't even get slick around the edges, Katherine thought cattily.

The door of Stephen's office opened and the supplier came out. He stopped on the threshold to shake hands. "Thanks, Stephen," he said. "I'll see you on my next trip, then."

The man said goodbye to Katherine, and to Irene. His eyes widened a little when he spotted Hilary, but he didn't say a word, because just then Stephen said, "Come in, Hilary," and stepped aside to hold the door for her.

He wasn't surprised to see her waiting there, Katherine realized. And yet, Irene's orders were strict, and she didn't interrupt his conferences to announce any casual caller, no matter who it was.

So that meant he had known she was coming. And if he wasn't having dinner with the supplier, after all, then was it Hilary he was planning to take to The Pinnacle tonight?

Katherine's breathing had become fast and shallow, and there was a sharp pain deep inside her chest. What was almost more agonizing was that she knew—*knew*—why she was reacting like this.

She was jealous.

For no good reason, she told herself. She was his wife, if only in name; she was the mother of his child. What did it matter if he took a woman to dinner? He had his reasons, and no doubt they were good ones. And he had made promises to Katherine—important promises. He was a man of his word. He wouldn't break those promises, any more than she would break the vows she had made to him.

But the fact was, Katherine admitted painfully, those promises were no longer enough to satisfy her. She wanted more than what he had pledged—much more than to be just his wife in name, just the mother of his child.

She wanted to be his love, the most important element of his life—as he had become the most important part of hers.

When had she crossed the line from liking him, respecting him, enjoying the time she spent with him—and let her feelings become something more?

Just when, she asked herself miserably, had she fallen in love with Stephen Osborne?

CHAPTER EIGHT

KATHERINE CERTAINLY didn't ignore Irene's question about signing her outgoing mail; she simply didn't hear it. She went back into her office, shut the door, turned her chair toward the window and stared blindly out at the skyline.

When had she grown to love him?

The reverberation of that question was not like the blast of a single explosion, but more like the rapid-fire beat of a snare drum against her nerves, each beat driving the certainty deeper.

It hadn't been love at first sight, or anything of the sort, that was sure. She barely remembered the first time they had met, but it must have been soon after she'd come to work for Rafe. Stephen had been just another face, one of the almost-nameless hundreds she was trying to keep straight in her first week on the job. And in a company where everyone used first names—even referring to the big boss as Rafe—who would suspect that a Stephen might be any more important than a John or a Scott or a Travis?

But she'd never forget their second meeting. She'd had Irene's job then, and Stephen had come in from his own office, down in research and development, to see his father. She'd kept him waiting, kicking his heels in the outer office, because he didn't have an appointment, and it was only when Rafe greeted him that she realized how seriously flawed her judgment had been.

A little later, after Stephen had left Rafe's office, Katherine had tiptoed in to defend herself. She hadn't been as insubordinate as Stephen must have made her sound, she told Rafe. He hadn't given her his last name; he'd merely instructed her to tell the boss that Stephen wanted to see him. But she'd been acting on Rafe's orders not to disturb him until he'd finished his telephone calls, so of course she hadn't let Stephen go straight in, and if Rafe wanted to fire her for not reading minds, he could go right ahead.

Rafe had shouted with laughter at the whole misunderstanding—and then he obviously put the entire episode out of his mind and went straight on with the letters he'd been dictating.

The next day, when Katherine sought Stephen out and rather stiffly apologized, he'd presented her with his business card—so she would never forget him again, he had said—and the first of those devastatingly warm smiles....

How could anyone not like the man? And it was impossible not to respect him, because no matter how frustrating things got, he didn't take his feelings out on others. He didn't demand good work; instead, he somehow made everyone want to give him their best. And he was always there to back up his people when things got rough.

That was exactly what he had done—almost automatically, and without even knowing the cause—when Travis had dumped her, Katherine realized. She'd felt worthless and battered and rejected, and Stephen had been kind to her. His actions, and his very attitude, had been soothing and reassuring and healing.

It was certainly no wonder that she had responded to that sort of treatment.

But had it been quite normal for her to react so strongly? she asked herself. Wasn't it a bit bizarre to recover from a lost love so quickly, to transfer feelings so easily to another man, no matter how kindly he'd treated her?

She was forced to look at another possibility. Maybe that transfer of affection hadn't been so sudden after all. Maybe the change had been going on even before the actual break with Travis. Could she honestly say that it had been her heart that Travis had injured? Or only her ego?

She found herself frowning as she thought it over. In the last few months she had seen little of Travis; he'd been immersed in business, trying hard to keep his sales figures high in order to win his coveted promotion—or, as Katherine now realized, avoiding her so he could pay court to Sherry instead. She'd told herself at the time that she understood the need and accepted it, that soon the pressure would be off and they could make up for the lost opportunities. But had it really bothered her all that much? Was it possible that her feelings for Travis had lessened as time went by? Had the love she thought she felt for him gradually become little more than habit? When she found out about his engagement, had the only real blow been the one dealt to her pride?

Had she been in love with Stephen even before Travis had dumped her?

I was lucky, she told herself. But the admission did not come easily. How could she have been such a fool not to realize what was happening?

She had let herself be deceived by professionalism, perhaps. Because so many of the things she shared with

Stephen were job-related, she hadn't even looked at the personal side, or let herself wonder about him as a man—consciously, at least. To do so would have violated the unspoken rules of the office, the code that had worked so well for so many months.

And perhaps she had been blinded by familiarity, as well. She was with Stephen so much of the time that it was easy to ignore the changes in her feelings—they'd come about so slowly.

But now, looking back with a new and clearer vision, she could see that with every passing day she had grown to care more about him. And sometime in these last few months, she had crossed the line from liking to loving, from respect to desire.

There had been such comfort for her, at Rafe's apartment on the night of Sherry's engagement party, just in being beside him. She'd thought at the time that almost anyone would have done; it was simply reassuring to have human company. But that hadn't been it at all. Only Stephen could have made her feel that way. Only Stephen—because she had already wanted him.

And so when he'd taken her home that night—

"I set it up," she whispered. It had been subconscious, but that didn't make the facts less real, or her responsibility less oppressive. She hadn't planned it out on paper, but she had orchestrated it nonetheless.

She hadn't anticipated all the results, of course. She hadn't planned on the baby.

But this sudden burst of honest appraisal of her motives forced her to admit that she hadn't done anything to prevent that outcome, either. She had no excuse for her carelessness; she was an intelligent woman who certainly knew better than to play Russian roulette.

And once again it had been Stephen who had stepped in to rescue her from the disastrous consequences— Stephen who had offered marriage...

Why had he done it?

His sense of responsibility, she told herself. He wasn't the sort of man who could walk away from a child.

But was there something else that had prompted him? More than once she had found herself thinking that there must be some other motive behind his actions, but she'd pushed that thought away. And though on the surface she, herself, had hesitated and expressed doubts, even encouraging him to think it over, the truth was that she'd leapt at his offer of marriage—because she'd desperately wanted to be his wife.

A perfunctory knock on the door was the only warning she had. Stephen was inside her office and standing beside her chair before Katherine could do much more than pull herself up straight.

"Are you all right?" he demanded. "Irene was worried."

"So she ran to you?" The question was almost nasty, and she instantly regretted it.

"It's not like you to be this way, Katherine. Do you think we should call Julie?"

"To diagnose a mood swing? I can do that myself." She swiveled her chair around so her back would be to the light. "I'm all right, just dead tired. I need to take a break."

He studied her face, and nodded. "Why don't you go home for a nap?"

And stay there alone all evening? Katherine thought. Wondering where he was, and what he was doing?

"No," she said. "I mean I need a change, not a rest." She was putting folders away without looking at him. "I think I'll go to the art museum to see the new show."

He moved then; she thought for a moment that he was leaving, but instead he circled her desk and dropped into a chair. "What's the show?"

"French impressionists." She closed the file drawer and turned to get her handbag.

"Mind if I tag along?"

She almost bumped her head on the credenza. "Why? Are you afraid I'm going to pass out?"

Stephen raised an eyebrow and countered coolly, "Is there any particular reason you don't want my company?"

"I wasn't saying that, exactly. From your opinion of the museum, I didn't think you were likely to be interested in impressionist paintings."

"I said I didn't like the building, not that I didn't appreciate what was inside. Did you make that reservation at The Pinnacle?"

"Yes." She found herself wishing she could cancel it.

He rose, lazily. "I'll have Irene change the time. After an hour of art, you may need that nap before dinner."

"You're—" Her voice was no more than a squeak. She cleared her throat and tried again. "You wanted the reservation for us?"

Stephen's eyes narrowed. "Yes, why shouldn't I? We did get good news today, remember?"

You didn't seem to want to celebrate then, she thought rebelliously. "I thought you were taking—" She stopped, and then finished lamely. "Someone else."

"The supplier is the beer-and-cheeseburger type, I'm afraid. I don't think he'd be comfortable at— Oh, I see." He smiled a little. "You ran into Hilary, and jumped to conclusions."

Katherine bit her lip miserably. Perhaps it *had* been a foolish assumption, born of her own jealousy and fed by her lack of self-confidence, and by the distant way he'd been acting earlier. Now that she thought it over, she realized that he surely wouldn't have flaunted Hilary in front of her at the office. If she had been thinking clearly, Katherine would have seen how silly the whole thing was—at least in time to keep her mouth shut instead of sharing her idiocy with him!

"She came to beg a donation for her favorite charity," Stephen said. "That's all. I'm beginning to think Rafe was right about the advantages of being a married man." He sounded rather self-satisfied.

Of course, Katherine told herself. That was the missing piece.

Stephen had indicated at Sherry's party that Hilary was growing more serious than he liked. Jake Holland had said much the same thing at the wedding, when he had mentioned Hilary laying matrimonial traps.

But now Stephen didn't need to worry about that any more, did he?

That was the hidden motive Katherine had sensed all along. She should have realized that one of the biggest advantages for Stephen in this whole affair was that no other woman could make demands on him, now that he was not only a married man but soon to be a father.

And at the same time, Katherine herself was in no position to ask for anything more than he'd already given her. She couldn't become a troublemaker, because she owed him too much.

What he'd offered, of course, was largely material; a house, a pink-and-blue nursery. He had no shortage of money, so that kind of gift cost him little in real terms. What he hadn't promised her was the personal side— things like understanding, shared hopes and dreams, and fidelity. He would spend enough time with her, she was certain, to maintain his image as a family man. He had as much as told her he would. But beyond that, if he was inclined to wander, Katherine could hardly make a fuss no matter what he did, even if she was actually to catch him with another woman.

The truth was, she wouldn't dare challenge him—not because she feared losing out materially, but because having *any* of his time, his attention, his concern, was better than having none at all.

Once she had said, severely, that she would never get involved with a married man, that she wanted better than that for herself. Now she knew why women sometimes gave up their freedom for relationships like that— and why they stayed.

It was ironic, of course, though no less painful, that the married man for whom she was giving up her freedom was her own husband. Her love for him would force her to be satisfied with whatever she could have, no matter how little it was.

Meanwhile, and more ironic yet, by giving up his freedom in order to marry Katherine, Stephen was actually freer than he'd ever been before.

SHE HAD TO FORCE herself to study the paintings. They were gorgeous, and it was impressive to see the glorious colors and the intricate brush work from mere inches away. But on this afternoon Katherine would have been just as intrigued by a comic book.

Stephen seemed to have no such problem. He strolled from gallery to gallery, hands in his trouser pockets, inspecting each painting with infinite care. "Look at this," he said once, pointing. "Van Gogh put the paint on his canvas so thickly I'll bet it's still wet underneath. That's what gives it that luminous glow."

Katherine dutifully admired the technique, then wandered off to stand almost unseeing before a bunch of tiny dots that, from a distance, formed a soft and hazy vine-covered cottage.

It wasn't fair. She was supposed to be enjoying this show, while Stephen should be floundering in the unfamiliar; as far as she knew, he set foot in the art museum no more than once a year.

But then, she reflected wryly, Stephen had an advantage in this case. He didn't have the same reaction to Katherine that she did to him—the almost suffocating sense of his presence and the sonarlike quiver that ran through her whenever he came close. He was free to concentrate on the art, while the only thing she really wanted to look at was him. . . .

Damn, she thought. *Things were a lot more comfortable this afternoon before I realized that I've fallen in love with him.*

So what could she do about it now? Not much, she admitted. She couldn't force him to return her feelings, or to change his attitude. Confronting him certainly wouldn't alter anything. Sulking, pouting or crying about her misfortune would only make matters worse. Then what was left? Accepting the reality of the situation and making the best of it, that was all. She could be pleasant, and decent, and keep her mood swings under control as much as possible—that was about it. But if she hoped for the best, rather than anticipating the worst, starting with the fact that she, not Hilary, was the one he was taking to dinner tonight—

She turned around, seeking him out, and was startled to find that he wasn't paying attention to the
paintings anymore. He was sitting on a low wooden
bench in the middle of the room, arms crossed, leaning
forward and intently watching a baby in a stroller a few
feet away. The baby, a girl Katherine guessed at about
a year old, was just as somberly staring back at him.

Katherine wondered what he was thinking. Was it
anticipation that was running through his mind just
now? Uneasiness? Fear? Regret? Some mixture of all of
them, most likely. She knew what that felt like, and a
little swell of sympathy touched her heart. This couldn't
be an easy adjustment for him, either.

She settled onto the bench beside him, at a careful
distance. "It's not your imagination," she said. "There
are more babies and pregnant women around this city
than there ever were before. I've decided there must be
a convention in town."

Katherine was astonished to see him turn just a little
red around the ears. "You too?" he said. "I thought I
was seeing things." He laid a hand over hers on the
bench. His fingers were warm, contrasting sharply with
the chilly wood surface under her palm. She hesitated
for a moment, then turned her hand under his until their
palms met and their fingers interlocked.

Was it sheer foolishness to think that reaching out to
him could cause anything more than increased pain in
the long run? She slowly lifted her gaze to meet his, and
saw the smile coming to life in his eyes.

I don't care, she thought. *For right now, this is
enough. And later, when it hurts—I'll worry about that
then.*

THE MAÎTRE D' at The Pinnacle was a professional, that was certain; though he greeted Stephen by name, he didn't by the flicker of an eyelash betray that he had ever seen him in the company of a woman other than Katherine. The waiter, however, was not as well disciplined. He blinked—twice—when Stephen told him that Mrs. Osborne wished to have the tournedos of beef, and had to ask a second time about her salad.

"You've given the poor man heart failure," Katherine accused, as soon as he was gone.

"The waiter?" Stephen didn't seem interested. "I'm sure it's not the first time he's had a surprise like that. Are you sure you don't want an appetizer?"

Katherine considered, and shook her head. "I'm starving, yes," she admitted. "But I want to enjoy my tournedos."

"I thought you said Jake gave you lunch."

"He did, but I wasn't very hungry then. And in any case, we got so involved in talking about your cellular telephone idea that I forgot to eat. Did you call him this afternoon?"

"I tried. He was out. What's the verdict on my idea?"

She propped her elbows on the edge of the table and rested her chin on her clasped hands. "Didn't you know? He's got the unit installed up at the estate he was working on in the mountains, and it seems to be fine. But he said the wiring is an additional nuisance."

Stephen frowned. "Not all that much worse than an ordinary connection."

"Still, it's one more unit to be hooked into the central computer. So I thought—I mean I wondered—" She was almost breathless. "Instead of buying a regular cellular telephone, why couldn't we build a stripped-down model right into the computer that operates the whole system? Jake thought it was a great idea. It would be one less connection to install, one less to break down or be interfered with. And if the telephone needs only limited capacity anyway, why pay for a unit that can do everything?"

"It would also be a feature nobody else offers," Stephen said.

"Exactly. They can copy our product, but only by plugging the different elements together. We've got a smooth, sleek, single package—easy to market." She sat back in her chair in triumph, and promptly ruined her self-confident image by adding anxiously, "What do you think?"

He picked up his salad fork and was drawing patterns on the linen tablecloth with the handle. "You might be onto something," he said slowly. "I'll have the research and development people take a look. If it works out, Katherine, you get the honors."

A little glow suffused her whole body. "Jake deserves some of the credit, too. I had the idea, but it never would have occurred to me if it wasn't for some of the things he said. He provided the atmosphere for the brainstorm, so—"

The waiter brought their salads. "It must have been quite a lunch," Stephen said idly. "Sorry I missed it."

Katherine tackled her spinach and tomato salad with enthusiasm. "Oh, it was great fun." She would have gone on to mention some of the other things she and Jake had talked about, but before she could finish her first bite, Stephen had changed the subject.

"We need to decide some particulars about a house right away, so that as soon as you're feeling better we can start to look around."

"There's no real hurry, is there?"

"If you're going to have the pink-and-blue nursery done by the first of April, there is."

Katherine looked at the tomato wedge that was speared on her fork as if she didn't quite know what it was. She was suddenly feeling sick again. But this wasn't her usual nausea, which she was almost getting used to, but a different, soul-deep ache.

It could have all been so perfect, she thought, *if this was only real.*

"What kind of a house would you like, Katherine?"

She stopped eating. Behind her napkin, she murmured, "It doesn't matter. It doesn't even have to be a house. Anywhere that has enough room will do."

Stephen looked at her long and thoughtfully. "Of course it matters. Did you think I was only asking to be polite, before I tell you what you can't have?"

She put her napkin down and said quietly, "I'm sure you have some ideas of what *you'd* like."

"I suppose I do," he said. "I will not abide one of those long rows of town houses, or any development, in which all the houses look identical. I absolutely refuse to count driveways in order to know which one to park my car in."

Katherine tried to smile. "You could put up a flagpole. Or plant a rosebush. Or paint the front door red."

"I could, but I don't plan to. Other than that restriction the choice is yours. Is there something wrong with your salad?"

Katherine shook her head and picked up her fork to make another try at eating.

"So, what does your ideal house look like, Katherine?"

She gave in. There was no reason on earth not to tell him, was there? "I've always wanted a red brick Colonial with white pillars and green shutters and a sun room and an attic. The kind of place that looks like it's been in the family for three hundred years and just grew slowly over time because no one ever threw anything good away. Is that different enough to please you? There are probably thousands of them."

"As long as they're not all on the same street, it's fine with me."

The waiter sighed over Katherine's uneaten salad and replaced it with the tournedos, small medallions of tender beef in a delicate sauce.

Stephen cut into his lamb chops. "I'm not surprised at your tastes, but I am curious. Is that the kind of house you grew up in?"

"Me?" Katherine said crisply. "Try a tract house in Fort Collins. Not only the house but the neighborhood had seen better days. A couple of men down the street had a car they raced, and they were always tinkering with the engine—generally after they worked the swing shift." And Stephen probably couldn't be less interested in her childhood, she reminded herself.

He smiled a little. "So you want a quiet neighborhood where the houses are far apart."

"At least where there's enough room to breathe—and so if a child gets noisy or defiant not everyone in the block can hear."

"Thick walls," Stephen added. "Ivy-covered, for extra soundproofing when we're beating the kid."

Katherine stared at him in astonishment, and caught the whimsical gleam in his eyes.

She was still laughing when she looked up and saw Travis and Sherry coming in. They were part of a small group following the maître d' toward a private party room at the back of the restaurant. It was the first time she had seen Travis since before her wedding, and catching sight of him was like being reminded of an old nightmare—one that was half-forgotten but still uncomfortable to think about.

Stephen followed her gaze just as Sherry saw them and broke away from the group to come over. Travis was two steps behind her; Katherine thought he looked a bit reluctant.

"The way you two have disappeared," Sherry said, without bothering to lower her voice, "it makes everyone wonder what you're hiding."

Stephen pushed his chair back and rose. "Some of us have work to do."

"Surely you don't need to keep Travis in perpetual motion, do you?" Sherry sounded sulky.

"I wasn't aware that I was," Stephen said mildly.

"I hardly see him anymore."

Travis spoke up. "I've told you, Sherry, I have a lot of new responsibilities."

Sherry shrugged and turned to Katherine. "I'll be chairing a designer showcase house next spring," she announced. "I'll tell the coordinators that you'll be helping me, if you'd like."

What sounded like a generous offer to share the limelight actually translated to a demand for free secretarial assistance, Katherine realized. "Thank you, Sherry, but I'm afraid I'll be too busy next spring."

Sherry's delicately arched eyebrows soared. "Surely you understand that chances like this don't come along often. In your position, Katherine, I should think you'd want to make your way in society."

"In Katherine's position," Stephen interrupted, "she may choose to do whatever she likes."

Sherry fussed with the ruffle that pretended to conceal the deep-slashed neckline of her glittery dress. "Well, if you want her to be a fuddy-duddy, Stephen..."

Travis eyed the gleam of diamonds on Katherine's left hand and said, under his breath, "I guess I was wrong. You do recognize your opportunities, don't you, Kathy?"

"Don't let us keep your friends waiting," Stephen said coolly. He sank back into his chair as soon as they were gone. "Sorry. Sometimes I think she was switched as a baby with the real Sherry Osborne."

"I'm sure the showcase house is a good cause."

"That's beside the point. Sherry has never learned the difference between asserting herself and being downright bossy."

Katherine pushed a bite of food around on her plate. "She doesn't know about the baby yet, does she?"

"I didn't see any particular reason to tell her."

"But you told Rafe."

"Rafe was a different case altogether."

Katherine thought that over for a minute. "Sherry wasn't very old when your mother died, was she?"

"About six. Why?"

"She must have been very hurt. When my mother died... But of course, I was old enough to be on my own then."

He picked up his wineglass. "You didn't have any family left?"

"Not really. My stepfather had a couple of sons from his previous marriage, but I didn't see them often. We never were much of a family."

"He never adopted you?"

"No. I suppose it was because my mother was getting a pension from the government for me. That isn't a very pretty picture, is it?"

"It happens. Was your father on active duty?"

"He wasn't killed in combat, no. He was on his way to his station in the Far East when his plane crashed. It was a big thing at the time—it wiped out his whole unit." She fidgeted a bit. "Not that I remember, actually. I was only three."

His hand covered hers, warmly.

Please, she thought, *don't offer me sympathy right now. I'll start to cry.*

He seemed to read the plea in her big hazel eyes. He picked up her hand and began stroking the back of it with the tip of his index finger. "Tell me," he said lazily, "in this pink-and-blue nursery, you aren't planning to drape the bassinet with rivers of white lace, are you?"

She smiled in relief. "Why?" she challenged. "Do you have a problem with white lace? It won't make a baby boy into a sissy, you know, any more than teaching a little girl the proper way to throw a baseball makes her a tomboy."

His eyes lit up. "I suppose you're going to teach her?"

"I certainly could."

With their momentary seriousness forgotten, they wrangled quite companionably over their after-dinner drinks—Stephen had coffee; Katherine, to the waiter's horror, asked for milk—and it was getting late when they went home.

She smothered a yawn in the elevator. She was relaxed and almost happy; it had been such a lovely evening. Surely she couldn't be alone in feeling that way, could she?

He took her coat to hang it up, and Katherine wandered into the living room and stood by the windows in the dark looking out at the golden lights of the city.

If attraction and affection and love had sneaked up on her, she thought, maybe it could happen to him as well. If she watched her moods, tried to keep things pleasant for him, made a home that he wanted to come to, then perhaps sooner or later—

He followed her into the room. She didn't turn, but she knew he was there, and her breathing quickened as he came to stand behind her, resting his hands on her shoulders and gently drawing her back against him.

Sooner or later—

"You sound as if you're ready to cry," he whispered.

Katherine shook her head.

His lips touched her temple, then traveled down across her cheekbone. He slowly pulled her hair away from her face and draped it over her ear so he could kiss the lobe, with its tiny golden topaz earring. She rested her head on his shoulder.

"Katherine," he murmured, almost against her lips. His hands slipped down over her shoulders until his arms were around her, cradling her to his chest.

She closed her eyes tightly against what promised to be an overwhelming assault on her senses—caused not only by his kiss but by her own longings. The expectation was correct; the soft brush of his mouth against hers sent quivers all the way to her toes.

How, she wondered, could a kiss that was so gentle—hardly more than a touch—cause such powerful reactions? She felt like a chocolate-dipped ice-cream cone on a hot afternoon; from the outside, she looked just the same, but if there was a single break in the delicate shell there would be no controlling the results.

And deep down inside her, that was precisely what Katherine wanted to happen.

Stephen raised his head, and she gasped a little, trying to refill her lungs. Her fingers clutched at his arms in an attempt to keep herself from sliding helplessly through his grasp—for her knees had no more strength to support her than would a life raft with no air in it.

Stephen shifted his grip, his arms tightening around her—not holding her captive, but keeping her safe, she thought. Relieved of the effort of holding herself upright, she sagged against him.

He kissed her temple again, and her hair, and said softly, "You look so tired, Katherine. Perhaps you should have had that nap after all."

She almost staggered with the surprise of it. Surely this was a beginning, not an end. If she told him now that she was not tired at all—

He released her slowly, balancing her with his hands on her shoulders. "I'm going to try calling Jake. He should be home by now. Good night, Katherine. Sleep well."

And as easily as that, she was dismissed.

She retreated to her room, trying to hold on to what dignity she still possessed, and as she brushed her hair she told herself that she had been a fool to pretend. Games like that were for children, and she was certainly not a child. She had only one option—to accept what she had been offered, and not to pin her hopes on more. She would only break her heart if she tried to fool herself into thinking that if she was sweet and nice, Stephen would eventually fall as much in love with her as she was with him.

That sort of thing only happened in fairy tales.

CHAPTER NINE

THE REAL ESTATE saleswoman looked rather sulky as she pulled the front door shut. While she dealt with putting the keys back in the security box attached to the doorknob, Katherine walked down the steps from portico to sidewalk and turned to stare at the house.

From the outside, it was a perfect red brick Colonial—so perfect that when they'd driven past it last night, she'd immediately told Stephen that she wanted to take the whole afternoon off to inspect it. It had white pillars, green shutters, a sun porch, an attic, a fenced back lawn—and it was one of only a half dozen houses on a quiet block.

But the inside was a different story. The rooms were tiny, cramped and dark. The kitchen was antique, the bathrooms primitive, and the second floor bedrooms were interconnected instead of having a hallway between. While Katherine agreed with the real estate saleswoman that all those things could indeed be fixed, she knew they couldn't be done by April, or for any reasonable budget.

Katherine was becoming discouraged. She'd looked at a dozen houses in the last couple of weeks, and not one of them came close to what she needed. "What's next?" she asked the saleswoman, who'd followed her to the front walk. "I have the rest of the afternoon."

The saleswoman dusted her hands together emphatically. "The truth is, I don't know what else to show you, Mrs. Osborne. You insisted on a Colonial, and you've looked at every one we've got and rejected them all."

"I never said that I would only buy a Colonial. You asked me what I liked, and I told you." Then she bit her tongue; it wasn't the woman's fault that the house Katherine wanted didn't seem to be on the market. "Maybe if I was to look through the listing books again—"

The saleswoman checked her watch. "I am sorry, but I have another appointment. Perhaps some other day."

Katherine studied her with a level gaze. And perhaps with some other sales representative as well, she thought. This one didn't seem to be taking her seriously.

Katherine walked down the peaceful little street, shuffling her feet through the crisp red and gold leaves that blanketed the sidewalk. It was a quiet neighborhood, though she'd seen evidence of children at several of the houses, and it was just the kind of street she would like to live on. But she knew she'd made the only possible decision. It was the middle of October already. By the time they got possession of the house, found an architect, finalized the plans, and hired a contractor to gut the place and start over, it would be Christmas—and not a stitch of actual work would have yet been done.

She got into her car and considered what to do with her unexpectedly free afternoon. She could go back to HomeSafe, of course, where there were plenty of details to keep her mind occupied, but she really didn't want to go back to work. She was feeling gloomy and disappointed and in need of consolation. Stephen was in Boulder in the midst of a conference about a new addition to the factory there, so she couldn't even tell him about this obstacle. Not that she would bother him with it during business hours, anyway. She was trying to be very careful about keeping personal things out of the office.

And that was not the only thing she was being cautious about these days, Katherine reflected. Despite the fact that she knew it was stupid and foolish and pointless, something deep inside her would not let go of the hope that she could in some measure control her own fate. And so she continued to play a desperate, superstitious variation of the old child's game. "Don't step on the crack," said the sidewalk chant, "or you'll break your mother's back!" Katherine's version was only slightly different. If just once she was less than kind and nice and pleasant, then Stephen would never love her at all. On the other hand, if she could only avoid all the cracks that loomed in her path . . .

But it wasn't easy to be cheerful all the time, to be pleasant no matter what went on, to be always deferential to Stephen's wishes, not to upset the situation, not to impose her own wishes—and she was tired of trying. Almighty tired, to tell the truth, of being cautious about everything she said and did.

She pounded her fist on the steering wheel in frustration; the violent action helped a little. It also shook down, from above the sun visor, the blurry ultrasound photograph of something that looked vaguely like an overgrown shrimp. She held the picture out at arms' length and squinted at it. She could see the baby's head, of course, but to her untrained eyes the rest was a blur, even though the technician had tried to point out the proper number of arms and legs. A very snub nose was the only facial feature she could make out, and she could see that much only because the baby had obligingly presented a profile view. There was certainly no telling whether her baby was a boy or a girl.

She smiled a little at the warm glow she felt at even this fuzzy image of the baby. She tucked the picture back up for safekeeping and turned her car toward her old neighborhood. Molly would like to see that photograph, and she would probably sympathize about the house, too. A cup of tea and a little gossip with Molly, and Katherine would feel a whole lot better.

She had hardly rung the bell when the door swung open a few inches. Alison's face lighted with delight, and she started to talk with one hand while she tried desperately to undo the security chain with the other. Katherine laughed and told her to slow down, but it was a futile effort. Once the door was fully open, Alison flung herself against Katherine for a bear hug and then led her triumphantly into the kitchen.

Molly looked up from a recipe book and smiled. "You're a nice surprise. With all the noise from my mixer, I didn't even hear the bell."

Puzzled, Katherine gave her a hug and said, "Then how did Alison know I rang it?"

"Oh, we've rigged up a light to flash when it rings. Want a bite of cookie dough?"

Absently, Katherine helped herself to a spoonful. "I never thought of problems like that."

"Few people do, as long as they have normal hearing. There are so many obstacles to a deaf person being entirely independent that it boggles the mind to think of them all."

Alison pulled up a chair and climbed onto it, wielding the biggest serving spoon Katherine had ever seen.

"I've never heard you sound so gloomy before," Katherine said.

Molly took Alison's big spoon away and handed her an ordinary one. "I'm not gloomy, really, just facing facts. Think about emergencies—there are telephones for the deaf, of course, but they only work if there's special equipment at both ends. And what if there's a community-wide disaster—a tornado or an earthquake or a chemical spill? Warning sirens won't do Alison any good, and neither will the radio."

Katherine shivered.

"I'm sorry," Molly said. "It's certainly not your fault, and here I'm letting you have it with my political routine. Being deaf isn't the worst thing that can happen, though I do think sometimes that almost any other disability would be easier to handle."

"That's not a lot of comfort, Molly. I already have nightmares about something being wrong with the baby."

"And I'm not helping matters, am I? How are you doing? You look great—your hair is so shiny and your face just glows."

Katherine's fingers plucked self-consciously at the lower edge of her loose sweater. "Do you think so? I'm beginning to get disdainful looks from people who suspect I'm letting myself go."

"Don't worry about it. They'll know the truth, soon enough."

Katherine found that comment less than encouraging. She held out the ultrasound blur. "First baby picture," she announced. "But baby did not want to cooperate, I'm afraid."

Molly studied it carefully, eyes narrowed. "It's a boy," she said, finally.

Katherine snatched it back. "Now how can you tell that? I've looked and looked. Even the technician said he couldn't tell for certain, and if he could, he wasn't allowed to say."

Molly grinned. "Wait and see."

"You guessed, I'll bet. That means you've got a fifty-fifty chance of being right."

"Maybe I guessed. And maybe I know." Molly removed Alison's spoon from the cookie dough once more, covered the bowl with plastic wrap, and set it into the refrigerator. "I promised Alison we'd walk down the street for ice cream this afternoon," she said. "Want to come along?"

Katherine nodded, and watched as Alison's eyes brightened in expectation. "She may not hear," she said, "but it looks to me as if she reads minds."

They strolled down the sidewalk, with Alison impatiently dancing along a few yards ahead of them, and talked about Katherine's so-far futile search for a house.

"I've got nursery furniture picked out, and nowhere to put it," she confided. "But if we buy a place that needs work, I'm afraid that just when I want to settle into my nest and not be bothered, I'm going to have a contractor demanding total involvement. And the prices are horrible, Molly."

Molly shrugged. "What does Stephen say?"

"He's not worried." *Sometimes I think that as long as we look like a happily married couple, he doesn't care what it costs him.*

The admission caused a hollow sort of feeling in the pit of her stomach. It was three weeks now since she had faced the truth of how much she loved him. Three weeks since that enchanted evening at The Pinnacle. Three weeks since that gently explosive kiss, which to him had obviously been nothing more than a good-night gesture—because since then, nothing had changed.

He still brought coffee to her room each morning, though the worst of the morning sickness had faded away with the passing time. He still looked after her with care, and sent her home if he thought she was growing tired. He still took her out for dinner, or brought home take-out food, or complimented her efforts when she did the cooking. And he still kissed her good-night—but they weren't the kind of kisses she longed for. They were nothing like that embrace three weeks ago....

To tell the truth, he was being so nice that it was driving her crazy. If she could just work up a healthy anger—but there was nothing to be angry about, really. It was hardly fair to be furious with the man because he didn't love her!

"I bet he's getting excited about the baby," Molly said.

Excited was too dramatic a term, Katherine thought. He had sat patiently through the ultrasound test, holding her hand and watching the monitor—interested, certainly, at what it showed. And concerned about her, and about the baby. But excited? She shook her head.

Molly's voice was soft and compassionate. "What's the matter, Katherine?"

Katherine stared straight ahead, fighting to keep the blur of tears out of her eyes. She'd never told Molly the whole truth, and she sure didn't want to break down and do it now.

It wasn't a good idea to come here after all, she thought.

A few yards in front of them, Alison had stopped near where a half dozen children were kicking a big rubber ball. As Katherine watched, the ball escaped, bouncing past Alison's outstretched hands and toward the street. Alison turned to go after it, single-minded, heedless of anything but her quarry.

Katherine started to scream, then realized it wouldn't do any good. Alison couldn't hear the warning. Molly broke into a run, but her action was as futile as Katherine's; she was too far away to stop her daughter before she reached the street.

Katherine closed her eyes when she heard the tortured shriek of brakes, but a few seconds later she realized that her imagination was worse than any reality could be, and in any case, Molly needed her right now.

She cautiously stole a look. The car had stopped, skewed in the center of the street. Past it, the ball still rolled, its motion slowing.

Alison stood on the curb, her body thrust forward and her toes over the edge, as if in the very act of stepping into the street she had remembered that she was never, never to do so—and had stopped.

The driver of the car came running. "Is she all right? That ball flew at me and then I saw her out of the corner of my eye—" He got a glimpse of Alison's face, brightly interested in the commotion, and oblivious to the extent of the danger she had been in, and swore. "Damn kids," he said. "Somebody ought to teach them a few things."

Molly turned Alison gently around and picked her up. Her face was white and her hands were shaking, but her voice was firm. "Somebody has," she pointed out quietly. "She stopped, didn't she?"

They walked on. Alison fidgeted a little, wanting down, but Molly held her securely. Outside the ice-cream shop, she sat on a picnic bench and patiently explained to the child what had happened, the danger she'd been in, and how happy Molly was that Alison had remembered what she'd been told and had not gone into the street.

Katherine watched in awe and shook her head. "I can't do it," she said. "I would have killed her. No explanations, no discussions—"

Molly gave her a slightly crooked smile. "No, you won't," she said. "What kind of ice cream would you like?"

And that, Katherine thought, was yet another example of Molly-style discipline: state the facts and move on to a distraction.

The whole incident left her shaken, and she was quieter than usual a couple of hours later when she left Molly and Alison and headed for home. Could she actually carry through with this? Could she honestly be a good parent? Was she only fooling herself to think she could handle it all?

But you don't have to handle it all, she reminded herself. She would have Stephen. . . .

But the fear of failure lingered, and it was a relief to run into Jake Holland in the lobby of the apartment tower. "Katherine!" he called, coming toward her. "I was just up to your door, trying to find Steve."

She glanced at her wristwatch. "He should be on his way home from Boulder now. Come and wait for him, if you like."

"You wouldn't mind? I really do need to talk to him."

"Not at all. I'm just going to make myself a snack."

Jake settled at the breakfast bar in the tiny kitchen and drank coffee while Katherine built herself a tremendous salad that included every fresh vegetable she could find in the refrigerator. It almost filled a small mixing bowl by the time she paused, and pouring herself a glass of orange juice she studied her handiwork. "Shredded cheese," she decided. "And slivered almonds on top."

Jake gazed at the bowl doubtfully. "Don't you think you're getting a little carried away?"

"Not as much as usual. I didn't feel like adding olives and turkey today." She found the almonds at the back of a cabinet and was starting to sprinkle them atop the salad greens when she saw a fleeting, puzzled look cross Jake's face.

Apparently, his befuddlement meant that Stephen hadn't shared the news about the baby with him yet. Katherine wasn't entirely surprised; considering what Jake had said about Hilary Clayton's attempts to trap Stephen into matrimony, she suspected he wouldn't pull his punches about this episode, either—at least to Stephen. Though she didn't think he would utter an ungentlemanly word directly to her, Katherine decided she'd rather not take the chance of hearing what Jake thought firsthand. She liked him too much to tell him half the story and allow him to think that she had planned and schemed and conspired to capture his friend—but she didn't know him well enough to trust him with the whole truth. If she let him discover her hopeless love for Stephen—

She added quickly, "Oh, you mean the sheer quantity of food here. Perhaps I did overdo it a bit, but I didn't have much for lunch. Would you like to share?" She divided the salad onto a pair of glass plates, pulled another stool up to the breakfast bar, and ladled low-calorie dressing onto her portion.

They talked about the new addition to the Boulder plant, about the progress the engineers were making with the built-in cellular telephone, and about the latest marketing campaign their competition had begun. But somewhere along the line, the conversation shifted from business to more personal matters, and Katherine found herself telling him about Alison, and the close call the child had had that afternoon.

"I saw the look on Molly's face," she said, with a shiver, "in the instant when she realized what was going to happen and knew that she absolutely could not stop it—that she couldn't reach Alison in time, and she couldn't get her attention."

Jake patted her shoulder. "Sounds to me as if Molly has everything under control. Give the child good training, and that's what comes through in a pinch."

Katherine was still not satisfied. "It doesn't always work out like that. If there had only been some way to call to her— But maybe there is," she mused. "If it's possible to rig up a flashing light to replace a doorbell, why couldn't something replace a warning shout?"

"I can see the poor kid now—walking around with a streetlight strapped to her back and every time she does something wrong it glares at her, just like Mom."

"Don't be silly. Maybe a light wouldn't work, but why not a vibration? Alison can feel that, I know, because there are songs she likes better than others, and it's the pattern of vibration that lets her tell the difference.'' She sat up straight, eyes glowing. "If computer chips can make talking wristwatches possible, Jake, why can't we make a tiny bracelet that vibrates when a transmitter is triggered from a distance?''

"Why stop at that?'' Jake drawled. "Make it an electrical shock instead. That ought to stop kids in their tracks.''

Katherine glared at him.

"You're serious, aren't you?'' he said.

"Absolutely. Tell me why it wouldn't work! It's just about the same principle as a garage door opener. Or any of HomeSafe's sensors.''

"I guess you're right. I'm not saying it *would* work," he added hastily. "But it does seem worth looking into.''

Katherine beamed, and flung her arms around him. "You're magical, Jake Holland, do you know that? Whenever I'm with you, incredible things happen!''

She had been so wrapped up in her line of argument that she hadn't heard the key in the front door, or the steady step on the quarry tile in the hallway. She didn't hear the kitchen door open. But she saw, from the corner of her eye, what could only be the gleam of a snow white shirt sleeve.

She turned her head in astonishment. Stephen was standing in the doorway, his dark red tie loose, his collar unbuttoned, the jacket of his charcoal suit slung over his shoulder.

"Oops," Jake Holland said.

Katherine was so close to him that the murmured word tickled her ear. She pulled abruptly away, struggling to keep her balance on the tall stool, and held her breath, half-fearful of the explosion to come. If Ste-

phen would only give her a chance to explain, to tell him
that it wasn't Jake's fault—

Stephen came across the kitchen. His kiss was a cool
brush against Katherine's cheek, just as usual. "Did the
house look promising, Katherine?"

Too stunned to open her mouth, she shook her head
automatically.

"That's a pity." Stephen held out a hand to Jake.
"Sorry you had to wait for me, Jake. Can I get you a
drink?"

Katherine's hands clenched on the edge of the breakfast bar, and she sat there for five full minutes after
Stephen had taken Jake into the living room.

Her mind was spinning in helpless circles, able to
comprehend only one fact: Her husband had walked in
as she embraced his best friend, and he had not even
cared.

Unless, she thought, Stephen had overheard what
they had been talking about, and realized that there was
nothing improper going on. Did his calmness mean he
knew Jake posed no threat to him?

She went back over the incident, trying to figure out
how long he could have been standing there. Not more
than a few seconds, she thought, for it was movement
that had caught her eye, and he couldn't have appeared
in the doorway without her being aware of it.

She could hear the murmur of voices in the living
room, but not the words. Surely if there had been anger in one of those voices, and self-defense in the other,
she would have heard it.

He trusts me, she told herself. But she wasn't convinced. If Stephen had interpreted that embrace as no
more than developing friendliness, wouldn't he have
made some teasing comment about it? Or would he

simply turn a blind eye altogether, rather than risk his friendship with Jake Holland?

"That would certainly tell you where you rank, wouldn't it, Katherine?" she muttered bitterly.

She sat there for a long time, trying almost desperately to convince herself that nothing had changed. "It doesn't matter," she told herself. "You'll have the baby. You can make that child the center of your world. And Stephen—you'll still be his wife, in name if nothing else. That's what you agreed to in the beginning. You haven't lost anything."

She could still love him. Whether he ever responded to her love or not, nothing could stop her from doing that. And what alternative did she have, anyway? To walk away from him altogether?

It was what she should do, she reflected. If she had the smallest speck of pride, she would go straight back to her room right now and pack her things.

But she knew she wouldn't—because even through her pain, she realized that being without him would be worse.

She heard Jake leave, and she listened to the friendly tones of their parting, and waited—but Stephen didn't come back to the kitchen. A few minutes later she slid off the high stool and went into the living room. Stephen was sitting in his favorite big chair with the evening paper on his knee.

He's the picture of contentment, she thought cynically. *If I'd only brought him his slippers everything would be perfect.*

He refolded the paper. "What was wrong with the house?"

"Almost everything." Her voice was clipped.

"Do you want to tell me about it?"

"The house? Not particularly."

His eyebrows rose a fraction. "If you think I'm waiting for an explanation of the scene in the kitchen, don't worry."

"Did Jake tell you what happened?"

"Yes, he did. But even if he hadn't, you wouldn't need to be concerned about it, Katherine."

His calm tone should have made her feel better, but it didn't. Instead, his words seemed to light a slow-burning fuse deep inside her. She moved toward the windows, where the last purple rays of sunset gleamed against the mountains. "Does that mean you trust me? Or that you trust Jake? Or that you don't care?"

He tossed the newspaper aside. "Katherine, if you were hugging Jake just to get a reaction out of me..."

She said bitterly, "Of course I wasn't. I don't think it's possible to make you react to anything."

"Would you be happier if I made a scene?" He followed her to the windows and turned her around to face him. Then his hand slipped from her shoulder to her chin and raised her face until he could look down into the liquid hazel of her eyes. She tried desperately to blink the tears away.

He said huskily, "Oh, dammit, Katherine. If things were only different—"

Even if she'd wanted to, she could not have side-stepped quickly enough to avoid the sweep of his arm pulling her close. But she didn't want to escape; instead, she relaxed against him, glad of the warmth of his body and the way she fitted so precisely against his solid chest, her cheek resting on his collarbone where she could feel the way his heart was pounding.

That alone was enough to give her hope.

He didn't make any move to kiss her. He just held her, so tightly that she would have protested, except that she couldn't bear it if he let her go. So she buried her face in the curve of his neck, and tried to think about what he had said, and what it might mean for their future.

It took raw effort to force herself to whisper, "What things, Stephen? And different—how?"

He rested his chin on top of her head. She couldn't see, but she imagined he must be staring out at the darkening skyline, where lights twinkled on one by one, and thinking—what? She held her breath.

And then he brushed a hand almost awkwardly down the length of her hair and let her go. "We have some things we have to talk about, Katherine."

She felt rejected, set aside, abandoned, and she was as stunned as if the floor had suddenly turned into a log raft adrift on a tumultuous sea. If whatever was bothering him was something he couldn't discuss while he was touching her, it was a heavy matter indeed, and that terrified her.

When the doorbell rang she didn't register for a moment what it was. Then Stephen said harshly, "Ignore it. Whoever it is will go away." They stood, tensely waiting to hear the sound of retreating footsteps.

But the bell rang again, longer this time, and a fist pounded against the door. "Dammit, Stephen, I know you're in there!"

"It's Sherry," Katherine said, surprised.

Stephen put a hand out to stop her, but she had already turned toward the hallway.

Sherry stalked in and flung her trench coat over the back of the nearest chair. Katherine was staggered by the change since the last time she had seen the woman;

Sherry looked ten years older. Her hair was windblown and her makeup was in desperate need of touching up. She stood with her arms folded across the front of her sweater, her chin at a defiant angle, and said to Stephen, "Thank you—I suppose."

"For what?" He sounded wary.

"For telling me that whatever Travis was doing with all his time, he wasn't working."

"I told you that?" Stephen waved a hand at a chair, inviting her to sit down.

Sherry ignored the gesture. "Not directly. But when you said it wasn't on your orders that he was working overtime, I started to wonder. I found him tonight with his little cupcake—the sales rep out in Boulder."

So that was why he was spending so much time in Boulder, Katherine thought. Travis hadn't been worried about accounts; it was affairs he had on his mind. "You poor dear," she said, and gave Sherry a comforting pat on the arm.

She meant it, too. In the long run, of course, Sherry was lucky to have found him out, as Katherine herself was. But that knowledge came slowly, as she knew from experience—and it didn't eliminate the immediate pain.

Sherry's eyes flashed with fury. She picked up her trench coat and slung it over her shoulders. "Don't twist your tongue giving me sympathy, Katherine," she snapped. "From the sound of things, you don't have a lot of room to talk."

Katherine felt an uncomfortable wave of color sweep up from her toes.

Sherry turned to Stephen. "Or haven't you heard that one yet?" she cooed. "There's a lovely rumor going round HomeSafe that Katherine's pregnant—that Travis is the baby's father, and Rafe made you marry her. How much of it is true, Stephen?'' She smiled at Katherine. "And just think, all this time, I thought it was Rafe you were after." She strode toward the front door.

Stephen caught her arm in a grip that was obviously painful. "I'll tell you what, Sherry. Let's make a deal. You don't feed that rumor, and I won't tell anyone what a fool you are—and I'm not talking about just this mess with Travis. I know a whole lot of things that you wouldn't want your society friends to hear."

Sherry winced. "All right," she said crossly, pulling away from him. "It's no problem for me to keep my mouth shut."

She tossed her head and marched out of the apartment.

In the sudden silence, Katherine thought, *It's all right. We're safe now.*

And then she realized uneasily that Stephen had reacted just a shade too quickly. There had not been even a split second of surprise or hesitation—she had sat in on too many negotiations with him to have missed it, no matter how well masked. And surely there should have been.

Unless...

If things were only different, he had said a few minutes ago. *We have to talk....*

Sherry's accusations had not been a shock to him, Katherine realized. He'd already known about her and Travis. He'd already heard the rumors.

And worse, he believed them.

CHAPTER TEN

SHE COULD SEE that belief in his eyes. And the compassion and sympathy. He wasn't angry, or shocked, or disappointed, for Sherry's accusation hadn't come as a surprise.

"I'm sorry," he said. "I didn't expect that to happen."

Katherine bit her lip until it felt numb from the pressure, and lifted her chin a little to look directly at him. "You were in Boulder today."

"My trip didn't have anything to do with that little scene."

"But it didn't exactly surprise you, did it?"

He sighed. "I knew about Travis, yes. But I didn't expect Sherry would have caught on just yet."

"And you knew about the rumors. Is that what you wanted to talk about? Travis and me?"

She thought he looked relieved at the level tone of her voice. She wasn't surprised; why should he realize how much pain was behind that quiet voice, how much fury was boiling up inside her? The crushing weight of helplessness was masking it even from her.

All she really knew was that she had never felt so alone in her life.

"Part of it," he said quietly.

But he didn't continue, and ultimately the silence was too much for her to bear. "How long have you known?"

"Months." He reached out as if to touch her shoulder.

Katherine jerked away from his outstretched hand. "How?"

Stephen's hand dropped to his side. "Little things, mostly."

"But that didn't stop you from taking advantage of me, did it, when the opportunity came up?" She wasn't being entirely fair, and she knew it, but the ache inside her was so great that the only way to lessen it was to strike out.

He flinched. "Katherine, you were in such pain that night...."

"And you felt sorry for me, I suppose?" Her voice was like a lash.

"Not exactly," he said quietly. "I was afraid for you. I thought for awhile on the terrace that you were going to throw yourself over the edge. So I made up my mind not to leave you—but things got out of hand, and ended up even worse."

"And then you were trapped," she said cynically.

"Trapped? No. Katherine, please give me credit for one thing. I have never tried to avoid my responsibility."

She frowned a little. "If you didn't think the baby was yours—"

"I certainly knew it could be."

She was rummaging through her memory, and coming up short. "Stephen," she accused, "you never even asked me if the baby was yours." It hadn't occurred to her before that the question, important as it was, had never come up in all their discussions of the child. She hadn't noticed the lack at the time; because there had been no uncertainty in her own mind, she had assumed that there was also none in his. But the fact remained that the question—the doubts—had never been expressed.

He shifted from one foot to the other, as if uneasy. "And I'm not asking now. It doesn't matter, Katherine."

"How generous of you," she mocked. "Of course, what that really means is that you wouldn't believe me if I told you—so why should I waste my breath?" She turned her back on him, fighting to keep what little self-control she still had.

What do I do now? she asked herself. Because, no matter what he said, it *did* matter. There were genetic tests; she could force him to admit, sooner or later, that the child she carried was indeed his—

But that, she realized, wasn't really the issue. The question of parentage was much less important than the one of trust. If he couldn't trust her, if he couldn't accept her word— *I can deal with the knowledge that he doesn't love me,* she told herself. She could even share his life, and his home, and his child, knowing that he would never love her in the way she loved him. But she couldn't live without trust. She could not share her life with a man who thought she would lie to him about such a fundamental thing.

For no matter what he said, it would make a difference. She could already see how his doubts had harmed them. The quiet way he had received Dr. Quinn's report that all was well, as if he didn't care. His lack of excitement over the ultrasound exam. The fact that he hadn't shared, even with his best friend, the news that he was to be a father.

"You haven't told anyone at all, have you?" she accused. "You've kept it to yourself, as if it's some kind of nightmare and you'll wake up soon. Except for Rafe—"

What was it he had said about his father? *Rafe is a different case,* that was it. If it hadn't been necessary to explain his action, he wouldn't even have confessed the truth to Rafe, she supposed.

Stephen sighed. "If you want pinpoint accuracy, Katherine, I might as well admit that I didn't tell Rafe, either. He told me, after he saw you at that ridiculous temporary job of yours."

"He guessed?" Color scorched her cheeks in a painful flood. "So when you came to the park that day—"

"I wasn't surprised by the news, no."

"How did he know?"

Stephen shrugged. "You'll have to ask him how he made his diagnosis. All I know is that he came into my office and sat down with his feet on the corner of my desk and lit that damned cigar of his. You've realized, haven't you, that he only fires it up when there's trouble brewing? He told me he'd seen you, and that in his opinion the last thing you were suffering from was flu."

There was a sarcastic edge to her voice. "Didn't you tell him it probably had nothing to do with you?"

"I didn't tell him anything. I wish you'd get over the idea that your attraction to Travis was any big secret."

Katherine had to fight for composure. "Rafe knew that, too?"

"Of course he did."

"Then why did he come to you?"

"He said he thought I might be interested. Since he did see us leave the party together—"

"He drew his own conclusions," Katherine whispered. Then another, even more horrible possibility occurred to her. "Or did he want you to marry me to save Sherry from humiliation?"

"Don't be ridiculous, Katherine."

She clenched her hands helplessly. "Well, I suppose Rafe's reasons don't really matter—the effect was the same, wasn't it?" No wonder Stephen had told her that she couldn't come back to work unless she married him. Rafe would have been furious....

Stephen's face had gone grim. "Rafe doesn't give me orders, Katherine."

"But he's great at making suggestions, isn't he? I wonder if that's why he's so set on you being there when the baby's born—because it will make you feel more like a real daddy?"

"Dammit, Katherine—"

She put her chin up and glared at him, eyes blazing. "I release you from all promises, all debts, and all obligations, Stephen. And I consider myself free of mine as well. Now if you'll leave me alone so I can pack, I'll be gone within an hour and you won't hear from me again."

He took two steps toward her and reached for her arms. "You can't do that."

Katherine sidestepped him. "You don't have a single thing to say about it," she snapped.

"You might be surprised. You're my wife, Katherine."

"That state of affairs can be changed."

"Nevertheless, it gives me certain rights."

"Such enthusiasm all of a sudden!" she mocked. "Oh, I see, now—you're worried about the way Rafe will react if I walk out. Well, don't fret. I'll explain to him that it's all my fault, and I'm sure he won't take it out on you." She spun on her heel and started down the hall toward her bedroom, then paused to fling one more barb over her shoulder. "After all, I certainly have nothing to lose—my reputation is gone already. It won't cost me anything to help whitewash yours!"

Stephen's voice pursued her, harsh and cynical. "As long as you're talking to Rafe, be sure to tell him I said he was right a year ago when he told me to fire you!"

She stopped, dead still, in the center of the hallway, and felt herself swaying in shock.

It was the last direction from which she would have expected an attack, the one aspect of her life Katherine would have sworn no one could challenge. She was good at her job. Everyone said so. Even in the midst of this cool, mixed-up marriage, Stephen had always been complimentary about her work. And as for Rafe, hadn't he told her when she'd worked for him that she was nearly indispensible—to him and to HomeSafe?

She groped for the wall to help support herself.

No! Rafe would never have made such a statement, and that left only one possibility—that Stephen would say or do anything right now if he thought it would hurt her. This was a side of him she had never seen before, and that fact steeled her resolve to leave. It would be better to be truly on her own than to subject her child to this.

She stumbled, unable to see clearly because of the tears in her eyes. She was totally alone now—more alone, actually, than she would have been if she had chosen a different road from the beginning. If she'd refused Stephen's proposal, or even if she'd decided never to tell him about their child, then she would have been able to delude herself with the belief that she could have had his support if she had only chosen to ask for it. And she could have told her child about his father with confidence.

But now both she and the baby had been rejected—flatly, finally, unfairly, and without cause—and now she couldn't even pretend that things might have been different if she had chosen another way.

I can do it, she told herself fiercely. *I will do it—alone. I can survive this, too.*

She grabbed an overnight bag from the closet shelf. She would take the bare necessities and go to Molly's apartment for now. There would be time later for gathering up all the rest of her belongings—if she still wanted them at all, tainted as they were with memories.

She didn't hear Stephen until he was in the doorway of her bedroom, standing with his hands braced against the frame, blocking the opening. "Katherine, I'm sorry. That was unforgivable." His voice was hoarse.

Katherine didn't look up. "Oh, it's my fault entirely," she said tightly. "I said I wanted a reaction from you. I got one—and I don't much like what I saw. Go to hell, Stephen."

He stayed planted in the doorway. "Don't be upset. It's not good for you."

She was dumping the contents of her dressing table helter-skelter into the bag. Her hands were shaking with fury. "You have got the audacity to tell me to stay calm?" She picked up the last item on the dressing table—a gold picture frame—and slammed it as hard as she could against the door beside him. He didn't even jump.

The frame hit the doorknob, shattering the glass and punching a hole through the blurry photograph of a young man in military uniform.

For what seemed like an eon, Katherine held the ravaged remnants of the frame as fragments of glass dropped onto the carpet, staring in horrified disbelief at what just a little while ago had been the only remembrance she had of her father. Now it was nothing more than meaningless scraps of metal, glass and paper.

She dropped the pieces because her hands were shaking too badly to hold them any longer, and sagged onto the edge of the bed, arms folded tightly across her chest. Her head was bowed, and sobs of almost animal intensity tore at her throat.

Stephen stepped across the broken glass and knelt beside her. "Katherine," he whispered. "Honey, please, don't do this to yourself. It can be fixed...."

She knew he was right, in a sense. This photograph was ruined, but she could take the fragments of the original out of the vault and go through the whole process of restoration once more. But that didn't take away the pain caused by the wanton, thoughtless destruction. It was like losing her father all over again—except that this time she had done it on purpose. And mixed in was the knowledge that *her* child was losing his father, as well...

She shuddered away from Stephen's touch. He stayed there quietly for a moment longer, then he got to his feet and left the room.

It was completely unreasonable to feel she'd been abandoned, when that was precisely what she had told him she wanted. But the suddenness of his leaving made her ache even more.

She huddled there, her throat raw, her head pounding, too lifeless even to fling herself down against the pillows. She had no idea how long it was before he once again appeared in the doorway.

She didn't look up, so she didn't see the package he was holding. "I was going to save this for a couple of weeks," he said. "Till your birthday. But maybe it will make you feel better."

Nothing, she almost told him, would ever make her feel better. Certainly no mere gift had the power to salve her pain.

But he sat down beside her, at a careful distance, and thrust the package at her. It was a flat rectangle, like a candy box, but a little larger.

She might as well humor him, Katherine thought dully. What difference did it make? Her head hurt too badly to get up and pack just now, anyway.

The box wasn't wrapped, it wasn't marked in any way. It was plain brown corrugated cardboard, sturdy and solid and not at all glamorous. She lifted the lid.

And stared in disbelief at a photograph of a young man in a military uniform. A young man whose face was not blurry or indistinct. A young man whose smile seemed to reach out like a mirror image of her own—

"Where did you get this?" she whispered.

"From the studio where it was taken. They still had the files."

"How—?" Her throat was so raw that every word hurt. "There was no mark on the original, nothing to say where it came from."

"As soon as I saw that terrible copy you had, I was intrigued." He waved a hand at the remnants, scattered on the carpet. "I was convinced there should be some way to get a better one."

She shook her head. "It was the best they could do."

"I realized that when you gave me the original to put in the vault." Stephen's fingertip brushed a lock of hair back from her face, tucking it behind her ear.

Katherine scarcely noticed.

"It was such a tiny picture," he said. "But it was a formal portrait, not a snapshot, and that meant a studio, so maybe the negatives still existed. That also meant perhaps it hadn't been the only picture taken." His voice was quiet, soothing, as if he were telling a bedtime story. "But I didn't know where to start looking, or even what your father's name was, for certain. I couldn't read the name tag on his uniform, and for all I knew your mother had changed your last name when she remarried. A hopeless quest, right?"

"It would seem so." Katherine was still staring at the photograph, at the clear dark eyes of the man she had longed to know. "But obviously it wasn't."

"You were right about the crash that killed your father," he said gently. "It *was* a big event. It made front pages all over the country. So it wasn't hard to find out where and when it happened, and get a list of the victims that included his full name. I discovered where he'd been stationed, and that he'd just been promoted. It seemed reasonable he would have had his picture taken with his brand-new rank showing, and that he wouldn't have gone far to find a photographer—so that gave me an idea of where to look, and the approximate date of the picture."

With the edge of her fingernail, Katherine traced the insignia on the uniform collar. "But . . ."

"Then it came down to finding every studio around the base, hoping that the one I wanted was still in business, and praying that someone would have been too conscientious, or busy, or lazy, to clean out the old files."

"That's incredible. The odds of finding the right one . . ."

Stephen shrugged. "I was lucky. The owner's father started the place, and he never threw anything away. So—here you are."

"But it's so clear, so perfect." She held it up at an angle to catch the light.

"What you had was just a preliminary print. Perhaps he sent a set to your mother so she could choose the one she wanted. It was never intended to be permanent. That's why it was so faded and worn—even aside from being ripped to shreds—that the restoration didn't work very well."

She sat there in silence for a full minute, and then she whispered, "Stephen, I don't know how to thank you."

He didn't answer, but he squeezed her hand briefly, and then put it carefully back in her lap.

Tears flooded her eyes again, a mixture of self-pity and sadness and grief for what could have been if things had only been a little different . . .

Hadn't Stephen said that, too, somewhere in the minutes before Sherry had arrived and the world blew apart? What he had meant was clear now.

If it wasn't for his doubts about the baby, Katherine thought, *I could still fight for him.* If he could do something like this, there had to be hope that someday things could be different—if only that awful lack of trust wasn't getting in the way.

And yet—was that what he'd meant? He had seemed
to be wishing they could be closer—and yet if there'd
been no baby, doubts or no doubts, there would have
been no marriage—nothing on which to build any kind
of closeness at all.

His voice had been almost wistful, she thought. It
hadn't held resentment, or anger, or bitterness....

"Stephen," she whispered. "Why didn't you ask me?
About the baby, I mean."

For a moment she didn't know if he'd heard her.
Then, finally, there was a sigh, and an almost inaudi-
ble response. "Because I was afraid of what you would
tell me."

The silence in the room was so intense that Katherine could hear the hum of the refrigerator, down the hall
and around the corner, as clearly as if she were standing next to it. If he actually meant that...

Her throat was tight and dry, and her voice was almost a croak. "You would trust me to tell you the
truth?"

He didn't look at her, but at his hands. "Yes. I
would."

All the blood seemed to have drained from her brain.
The sensation made it even more difficult to grasp the
incredible implications of that statement. For if he
honestly believed that she wouldn't lie to him, even if
the answer was one he didn't want to hear—then anything was possible.

"I hoped the baby was mine," he went on quietly.
"And as long as I didn't know differently, then I didn't
have to face the questions that knowledge would bring."
He raised his head and looked at her, a quick, sidelong
glance. "I won't say I didn't wrestle with it for awhile,

Katherine. But then I realized that it didn't matter. It honestly didn't matter. You needed me, and I . . ."

The hope that had been slowly trickling into her heart drained away in a gush. "So you married me because you felt sorry for me, having to cope all by myself. And maybe a little guilty, too, because you slept with me once."

"Of course I felt guilty." His voice was low, almost painful. "I knew how unhappy you were. I knew you were only looking for comfort that night. But when you offered me all that gloriously lovely warmth of yours— I couldn't stop myself, Katherine. When you're suddenly offered what you've wanted for months—for years—sometimes you don't think very clearly about the consequences of taking it."

Katherine thought for a moment that her heart had stopped beating. There was a painful hollow in her chest.

"Fate handed you to me that night, gift-wrapped. And I'd had just enough champagne to let myself hope that you were real, that you meant it—that perhaps you weren't so deeply involved with Travis as I'd thought. At least you were seeing me, for a change. Me, not the boss—and you seemed to want me as much right then as I wanted you."

The room was starting to spin around her. Katherine carefully put her hands out and braced them against the mattress.

"But then the morning came, and you ran from me." He turned to scowl at her, his brown eyes brilliant with anger—and perhaps something else. "Is it any wonder I feel guilty? It was obvious that you hated me for what I'd done. You couldn't wait to get away from me. You even quit a job you loved just so you wouldn't have to look at me again—"

Her voice was ragged. "You wanted me to go!"

"No. I just didn't want to hurt you any more than I already had." He put his head down into his hands. "I loved you too much to do that."

And I, she thought humbly, *actually believed that he was capable of using me.* She had found motives where none existed, and now, finally, she understood why. All her life she'd known men who used rather than loved, and she had thought Stephen must be the same.

"But when I found out you were pregnant, I couldn't let you go through that alone."

She tried to reach out to him, but her hands were trembling so hard that she couldn't control her movements. "Even when you aren't sure the baby is yours?"

He raised his head. His voice was almost harsh. "I told you it doesn't matter. As far as he will ever know, I am his father. And that's enough for me, Katherine. That—and having you. Even if you can never exactly love me..."

It was a beautiful gift—a treasure of love that she would hold always close to her heart. She put her arms around him, and he buried his face in the curve of her neck, against the spill of golden brown hair.

"I was too stupid to realize it that night," she whispered. "But somewhere deep inside I must have known even then that it was you I loved."

He raised his head, and the blazing glory in his eyes sent startled anticipation shivering along Katherine's nerves.

"I have certainly never behaved that way before," she continued. "I never realized that I knew how to seduce a man..."

"I'm sure it's easier when he doesn't put up much of a fight." His fingers slipped slowly through her hair, pulling it back away from her face and cupping her head securely. "But any time you feel a need to practice, I'm available."

Katherine's stomach did flip-flops at the sultry promise. His mouth against hers took away any need for words, and by the time he let her go again, Katherine could hardly manage to say, "I thought you didn't even want to touch me."

He drew his fingers through her hair. "I was too afraid of losing control again to take a chance. And I wanted you too much to risk pushing you back into that shell of yours. I hoped if I could only wait long enough—"

"Foolish," she whispered.

"Maybe. But you're not the only one who would have liked a little human reaction now and then. Dammit, Katherine, whenever I tried to kiss you, you just got more polite. Or else you yawned in my face." He pulled her down with him against the satin. "I'd have had to be a brute to try to take you to bed when you were exhausted all the time."

That reminded her of things that were yet unsettled. The sooner they were made clear, she thought, the better.

"About the baby, Stephen," she said firmly.

His arms were around her, and she could feel the momentary tensing of his muscles.

"Do you really believe that I could have married you, carrying another man's child, and not told you?"

"No," he said. "In fact, it hadn't even occurred to me that you might, until Julie said the baby was due the first of April, not the middle."

Katherine's eyes dilated in shock. It was no wonder he hadn't been full of excited plans the day he had got that news, she thought. No wonder there had been no more baby books or stuffed elephants....

"And then once I started wondering, I remembered all kinds of little things that fit right in. You'd been dizzy at Sherry's party..."

She remembered that, now. "I hadn't eaten all day. And if there's a problem with the date, it's in Julie's charts, because I told her precisely when this baby was conceived. And believe me, I do know—" Suddenly she was once more almost on the edge of tears. "Oh, Stephen, I want so much for you to be excited—to be happy about our baby! Please, for my sake, will you try?"

He drew her closer. "I am, darling. Watching the little guy on the ultrasound monitor—I wanted to shout. I could have bought out a whole toy store, but I was afraid to—scared you felt trapped, not only with the baby but with me. When you cried over that baby book... And after all, you're the one who has morning sickness and backaches—"

She smiled mistily up at him. "And mood swings."

"Well, you're not the only one suffering from those. When I saw for myself how much you enjoyed being with Jake, and it seemed you could barely tolerate me—" His arms tightened possessively. "And when I'd bring you coffee every morning and have to look at those nightshirts of yours—"

"What's wrong with my nightshirts?"

"Nothing, love. That's the problem. Sound asleep in a flannel nightshirt you're sexier than most women in red satin."

She tipped her head up and gave her hair a shake. "And how much do you know about women in red satin?"

"Well . . . there were all those women I was continually parading through my office, trying to make you jealous. Or were you actually so oblivious that you didn't notice?" He sighed. "Dammit, Rafe was right. I should have fired you."

"You will never make me believe Rafe said that!"

Stephen held her a little way off from him. "He most certainly did. In fact, he offered to do it himself before he retired."

She didn't quite know whether to be hurt or offended. "If he thought I wasn't doing my job—"

"He thought you were doing it a great deal too well, and he told me if I wanted you to ever take me seriously, I'd get you out of my office. He also warned me that if I insisted on giving you that blasted promotion, I'd never get close to you, and that you'd still be distantly pleasant to me at our mutual retirement party."

"Oh," she said. "Well, I'll do my best. To be pleasant to you, I mean."

He looked down at her, eyes narrowed. "If you ever revert to the way you used to treat me, I will rip your clothes off in my office."

"Mr. Osborne," she murmured, "you do have a way with threats."

He pulled her close to him with a groan. "We've gone about everything backward, haven't we?" he mused.

"I'm sorry, love. I swear you'll get the courtship you deserve, Katherine—even if it takes the rest of my life."

She smiled up at him, and rubbed her cheek against his shoulder like a contented kitten, safe in the circle of his arms—and safe, for always, in his heart.

"Oh, it will," she murmured. "You can plan on it."

EPILOGUE

RAFE'S FINGERS TIGHTENED on the arms of his chair as the doctor came across the small waiting room. It was apparent that she was coming to talk to him, for he was the only one there at the moment; fathers' lounges outside maternity wings no longer were the busy places they once had been.

But a few minutes later, after Julie Quinn had given him the news, he didn't go in to join the new little family. There would be plenty of time for that, later. Instead, he strolled outside into a soft and silent April snowstorm, and paused to light the cigar he'd been nervously chewing since well before midnight.

It hadn't come off quite the way he had designed it, that was true. But it was close enough to satisfy him. In fact, he reflected, it was one of the better deals he'd put together in a long career of negotiation and compromise and flat-out manipulation. It was just too bad he couldn't sell stock in it.

Though as far as that was concerned, a seven-pound grandson wasn't a bad profit at all. He was contented with that.

Besides, with the way Stephen and Katherine were looking at each other these days—ever since they'd gone off to Hawaii last fall, as a matter of fact—there was the promise of another baby someday. Maybe it would be a girl next time.

A lighter streak slowly grew in the eastern sky as dawn approached, and Rafe Osborne smiled as he walked through the snow.

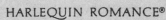

HARLEQUIN ROMANCE®

**Harlequin Romance
makes love
an adventure!**

Don't miss
next month's
exciting story in

THE BRIDAL COLLECTION

RESCUED BY LOVE
by Anne Marie Duquette

THE BRIDE wanted a new future.
THE GROOM was haunted by his past.
THEIR WEDDING was a Grand affair!

Available this month in
The Bridal Collection:
A BRIDE FOR RANSOM
by Renee Roszel
Harlequin Romance #3251
Wherever Harlequin books are sold.

WED-11

Where do you find hot Texas nights, smooth Texas charm and dangerously sexy cowboys?

DEEP IN THE HEART

Wedding Bells—Texas Style!

Even a Boston blue blood needs a Texas education. Ranch owner J. T. McKinney is handsome, strong, opinionated and totally charming. And he is determined to marry beautiful Bostonian Cynthia Page. However, the couple soon discovers a Texas cattleman's idea of marriage differs greatly from a New England career woman's!

CRYSTAL CREEK reverberates with the exciting rhythm of Texas. Each story features the rugged individuals who live and love in the Lone Star State. And each one ends with the same invitation...

Y'ALL COME BACK...REAL SOON!

Don't miss *DEEP IN THE HEART* by Barbara Kaye. Available in March wherever Harlequin books are sold.

CC-1

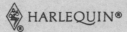

HARLEQUIN®

my Valentine

1993

The most romantic day of the year is here! Escape into the exquisite world of love with MY VALENTINE 1993. What better way to celebrate Valentine's Day than with this very romantic, sensuous collection of four original short stories, written by some of Harlequin's most popular authors.

**ANNE STUART
JUDITH ARNOLD
ANNE McALLISTER
LINDA RANDALL WISDOM**

**THIS VALENTINE'S DAY, DISCOVER ROMANCE
WITH MY VALENTINE 1993**

Available in February wherever Harlequin Books are sold.　　VAL93